# MAKING WAVES

# MAKING WAVES

## NICOLE LEIGH SHEPHERD

a *Pretty Tough* novel

razOr
bill

An Imprint of Penguin Group (USA) Inc.

Making Waves

RAZORBILL

Published by the Penguin Group
Penguin Young Readers Group
345 Hudson Street, New York, New York 10014, U.S.A.
Penguin Group (USA) Inc., 375 Hudson Street,
New York, New York 10014, U.S.A.
Penguin Group (Canada), 90 Eglinton Avenue East, Suite 700,
Toronto, Ontario, Canada M4P 2Y3 (a division of Pearson Penguin Canada Inc.)
Penguin Books Ltd, 80 Strand, London WC2R 0RL, England
Penguin Ireland, 25 St Stephen's Green, Dublin 2, Ireland
(a division of Penguin Books Ltd)
Penguin Group (Australia), 250 Camberwell Road, Camberwell, Victoria 3124,
Australia (a division of Pearson Australia Group Pty Ltd)
Penguin Books India Pvt Ltd, 11 Community Centre,
Panchsheel Park, New Delhi – 110 017, India
Penguin Group (NZ), 67 Apollo Drive, Rosedale,
Auckland 0632, New Zealand (a division of Pearson New Zealand Ltd)
Penguin Books (South Africa) (Pty) Ltd, 24 Sturdee Avenue,
Rosebank, Johannesburg 2196, South Africa

Penguin Books Ltd, Registered Offices: 80 Strand, London WC2R 0RL, England

10 9 8 7 6 5 4 3 2 1

ISBN 978-1-59514-415-7

Library of Congress Cataloging-in-Publication Data is available

Printed in the United States of America

To Justin Michael

# Chapter One

**"Freshman year is o-v-e-r!"** my best friend, Zoe Murphy, chants as we step out onto the slate pool deck after school lets out early for our first official day of summer vacation. Just a few hundred feet away, the Pacific Ocean stretches toward the horizon to Hawaii and beyond.

"Race you to the first chair," I say, taking off across the people-peppered deck. As I suck in the thick salty air, I pass country club members fanning themselves with hundred dollar bills.

Well, not exactly. But pretty close.

I reach the nearest canvas lounge chair in a matter of seconds and turn around expecting to spot Zoe right behind me. I'm surprised to find her strolling lazily across the stone path as if it's no big deal to be here at the Beachwood Country Club.

I guess for her, it isn't.

Personally, I can't believe I'm back at the beach. My beach. The one where I learned to swim as a kid. And that to top it all off, I'll be working here for the entire summer.

As I wait for Zoe to catch up, I run my fingers along the cool canvas chair and take in the sounds I've yearned to hear since I tore open my BCC congratulations letter two days ago. Seagulls cry above me and I can make out the faint cheers of a volleyball game to my right. I stare out at the surf crashing against the sand and imagine how great it will feel to be out there lifeguarding every day. It's been my dream since I was a little kid playing on this very beach.

My reverie is interrupted when Zoe finally catches up to me. "What are you looking at?" she asks, glancing briefly at the waves before turning to face me.

"Oh, nothing," I quickly reply. If she can look out at the ocean as if it's "just another" seaside scene, then I doubt I can make her understand how amazing it feels to be back at the beach I used to visit all the time before it was taken over by the club. "What's up with you this morning? Not in the mood to race?" I ask, shifting the conversation back to her.

"Not worth it. Abby Berkeley always wins," Zoe falls into the lounge chair next to me. "It's getting old."

"Whatever." I gingerly sit down on the reclined chair, my thoughts drifting to the time when I didn't win: when I discovered that Brody—the guy who I thought was the best ever, the one who I met at the swim meet in May, the one who I stayed up all night talking to, the guy whose lingering kiss sent shivers down my spine—wasn't interested in me.

Zoe sighs as she soaks in the Malibu sun. The noise forces me to remind myself that, as much as I don't want to admit it, Brody is a thing of the past. I need to concentrate on the stuff that matters now. Like my lifeguarding job.

I glance over in Zoe's direction. She stretches her gymnast-sized legs out, her toes barely reaching the other end of the chair.

"So I guess you don't want to go surfing?" I ask, eager to let the water drive away all thoughts of Brody.

"Not yet. Soon," she replies. "For now I just want to relax. After that all-night cram session for this morning's history final, I'm grouchier than Oscar."

"Oscar, really? Someone is watching a little too much *Sesame Street*."

"Me? You're the one who babysits like crazy," Zoe retorts.

She's right. I am the one to usually take the jobs. And lately, Zoe and I have been offered so many babysitting gigs that we'd been hoping to turn our sitting jobs into some serious summer cash and maybe even an official business. But with the club forcing me to work at the snack bar as a condition of my lifeguarding, the big question is whether I'll still have time to babysit.

Zoe places a pesky strand of brown hair behind her left ear and peeks out at me from beneath her Dior sunglasses. "Something wrong?" she asks.

I decide now's not the time to concern myself with trivial things like the Sunset Snack Bar. "I still can't get over how crazy it is that we're about to attend our first official lifeguard meeting!" I exclaim, hoping my glee will mask my worries. "You know, two o'clock is rapidly approaching."

"It is. And have I told you what a pioneer you are? I think you're the first non–club member to ever man a lifeguard chair here. You should be so prou— " She stops herself mid-word. "Wait. That came out wrong. I didn't mean . . ."

I hold up my hand. "Seriously, Zo? We've been friends long enough for you to know it takes a lot more to offend me. I live with three big-mouthed brothers," I say, fiddling with the navy visitor badge on my bag. "And honestly, even if you do decide to become all hoity-toity this summer because we're at your fancy-schmancy club, it's still better than dealing with the drama of softball season."

"Well, you know . . ." Zoe pauses, lowering her sunglasses to the bridge of her nose as a joke. "I'll try to keep the snootiness in check." She pushes her sunglasses back to their original position. "But let me just say 'amen to that, sister.' Basketball was bad this winter, but softball was really the worst. Between everything that went on with Amber and Kylie, and my brother and Kylie's big breakup, the season was messier than . . ." Zoe's voice trails off, her eyes drifting to my knee.

"I know. I know. You can say it. Messier than the spill I took at the school softball game last month." I grimace just thinking about the pain.

"Thank God it wasn't your ACL," Zoe replies, leaning over to squeeze my hand.

"No, thank goodness my bestie was there with me!" I grin from ear to ear and jump out of the chair, nearly knocking it over. "And, you know, that my knee is feeling better," I add sheepishly. I swiftly put the chair back into place, hoping that the BCC secret police don't notice my super classy maneuver. "Now, enough of this. Wanna hit the waves?"

"Always." Zoe pops out of her chair and motions for me to follow her toward the beach.

I squat down and carefully place my friendship necklace in my bag. Zoe leaves her matching one around her neck as she sets off for the water. We've been wearing the necklaces ever since one day in fourth grade when Zoe surprised me at school. They're from Tiffany's. Not that I care.

Practically skipping with excitement, we make our way to the ocean. Along the way, we pass a sparkling Olympic-sized pool with a separated lap section, a smaller round kiddie pool, and a Spanish-tiled Jacuzzi. At the kiddie pool, a stunning blonde woman waves at Zoe while balancing a plump baby on her lap.

Zoe smiles and waves back. She whispers "possible client" to me as we walk down the marble steps past the Sunset Snack Bar. I can't help but notice that my future place of employment looks nothing like the snack bar at my local swim club. That was pretty much just an orange umbrella over an ice cream–filled metal refrigerated box.

Zoe, meanwhile, doesn't even glance, much less gawk, at anything, not even the attached beverage bar offering everything from fresh fruit smoothies to ice-blends and exotic drinks.

When we reach the far end of the complex—and with it the Murphy's private cabana—Zoe grabs her brother Zach's longboard from its resting place against the white wooden siding and hands it to me.

I attach the longboard's velcro band around my ankle and find myself thinking about the last time I surfed . . . the day after I met

Brody. I gulp and quickly begin rubbing wax over the board, hoping that Zoe won't notice the frown that has just fallen across my face.

Naturally, I look up to find Zoe staring at me curiously. "I'm going to take a wild guess here and say that you're thinking about your one night stand," she says, raising her eyebrows conspiratorially.

"What?! I've never had a one night stand," I screech. I've always heeded my brothers' warnings about guys. I'd never cross that line. I gather up my board and abruptly leave the cabana.

"Come on, Abby. You know what I mean." Despite our height difference, Zoe keeps pace with me stride for stride. "Do you think you'll ever see him again?" she asks, looking up at me.

"Who?" I ask, acting oblivious.

"You know who. Your mystery boy."

I don't respond right away and for a few seconds we march to the water in silence. Passing a group of B-Dubbers playing volleyball, we each manage to muster a wave—our basketball bud Tamika is among the players—but neither of our hearts is really in it.

"Abby, seriously," Zoe implores. "Do you think you're destined to meet again?"

"Doubtful." I feel the familiar sting in my stomach as I charge ahead of Zoe.

Once we reach the surf, we wade in ankle-deep water for a few seconds, wetting our boards. I shake my leg, dislodging a piece of brown kelp from my ankle.

"That sucks that he left early for college."

I lay my board on the surface of the water. "I should have listened to my brothers. They're the ones who always told me that guys are only after one thing. And let's face it, after what happened with Nick—you know, making out and never calling me again—it's obvious that they're right."

"I don't know. Given what you told me about how you and he-who-shall-not-be-named shared a 'deep, emotional connection' and how you 'stayed up all night talking for hours that felt like mere moments' and how 'when you looked into his eyes, you finally believed in sappy love songs'—given all that, it just doesn't seem to me that he's the kind to kiss and bail."

"Why? Nick did." I say, ducking underneath a shallow wave. The chilliness of the water catches me by surprise and I quickly pop to the surface.

"The guy who you told me about doesn't sound a lot like Nick. What makes you think that he'd do the same thing?" Zoe pulls herself onto her board.

"Because he's a guy. And because once he realized that he wasn't going to score, he made up some lame-o excuse so he didn't have to see me again. Anyway, enough of this, I've moved on." I squeeze the edges of my board.

"Abs, I know you don't want to hear this, but it wasn't really a lame excuse. He said he was going to Michigan and that he didn't want to carry on a long-distance relationship in college. That's a pretty good reason."

"Yeah, a pretty good reason to get with college girls."

"Now you really do sound like your brothers." Zoe says, straddling her board.

"Well, unfortunately, unlike them I'm not a cop. I can't have him arrested."

"You *really* think they could have him arrested?"

"Yeah." Lying across the board, I begin to paddle through the chilly waves.

"On what grounds?" Zoe's board rises and falls along with a gentle wave.

"Overall jerkiness and refusal to commit."

"If those are your grounds, then they'd have to arrest almost every guy out there!"

"Well, then maybe I'm onto something." I lift myself up so that I'm sitting on my board.

"You're ridiculous. At least the conference wasn't a total wash. You stayed at a nice hotel. You got to go to San Fran. And you went home with first place medals for both butterfly and breaststroke. That's something."

"Yeah, I guess. . . ." I stare at a couple of surfers in the distance as the current moves me gently forward.

"I bet you probably wouldn't have gotten the job here this summer if you hadn't done so well there. Like I said, you're the first . . ."

"Non-member to lifeguard at the club. Don't remind me."

"I would think that knowing you, you'd see that as a call to arms, a reason to be the best lifeguard in the place."

"Oh, I am. Don't be confused about that. If there's any way to prove that I'm the top swimmer here, I'm going to do it." I sit up straighter.

"You'll be happy to know that there is."

"There is?"

"Yeah, they hold a yearly competition, the Last Blast." Zoe leans forward and paddles my way. "We had the joy of watching Zach compete last year when he was a lifeguard."

"Really? Sweet. If you'd just told me that to begin with—the competition part, not the Zach part—then I wouldn't have wasted your time talking about B—" I cut myself off.

"Ooh, a first inish . . ." Zoe claps her hands in excitement. "Have I mentioned how ridiculous it is that you won't tell me the guy's name? Let me take a guess: Is it Ben? Brad? Brent? Brandon? Bernard?"

"Bernard? Really? You think the boy of my dreams is named 'Bernard?'" I ask, adjusting the band on my ankle that attaches me to the longboard.

"Never mind. That's not important. What's important is that you need to talk to *someone* about him. Just because your family is super into 'keeping it all inside' doesn't mean that you should too. And to tell you the truth, I'd rather hear how you feel about some super sweet guy than hear you babble endlessly about winning."

"I don't babble."

"You babble."

"Well, I like winning." I shrug.

"I know. You've made that clear since kindergarten."

"Fine, so if you don't want me to talk about how I'm going to crush the competition this summer—*and I am*—and if I don't want to talk about you-know-who, then what *do* you want to talk about?"

"How about how there's plenty of fish in the sea?" Zoe glances around and points behind her to a surfer in the distance. "Like that guy," she says.

I don't turn around to see who she means. "Zoe, I told you, I don't want to hear about guys." I spot a wave and furiously paddle, deciding that if I'm going to be out in the ocean, I might as well have fun. As the wave pushes me forward, I spring to my feet, shifting my weight to balance on the board. Riding the momentum, I drop into the barrel and glide as if I'm skimming air, feeling the familiar adrenaline rush kick in.

And that's exactly when I see him. The surfer Zoe was talking about.

He looks exactly like Brody.

I lose my balance and crash into the water.

So much for moving on.

# Chapter Two

**Zoe and I catch** four-to-five-foot waves for about an hour, during which I look over my shoulder at least ten times to confirm that the surfer in question is just a Brody look-alike.

Eventually, we decide to call it quits so that we're in time for the information session. We paddle side-by-side back to shore until the water becomes too shallow. Then we gather up our boards and step out onto the warm sand, the grains crunching beneath our toes.

"You're so amazing in the water. With you here, the other lifeguards will probably just give up their whistles and buoys and call it a day," Zoe announces as the crashing of the ocean waves gives way to the sounds of our Beachwood Academy classmates enjoying their first few hours of summer vacation.

"Thanks," I say, avoiding washed up kelp. "I didn't realize how much I missed this beach." I look around at the members lounging on beach chairs. In the distance, I can see moms swimming in the pool with their kids, their coiffed heads held high above water. Beyond them, a few execs—who are clearly home early to enjoy the cloudless Southern California day—sit at the bar with chilled martinis beside them.

"I bet it's really different from what you remember," Zoe says.

"You can say that again."

"I bet it's really different from what . . ."

We burst out into a giggle fit.

When we reach our lounge chairs, Zoe grabs one of the white fluffy towels left out for us by a pool attendant and tosses it my way. Then she digs into her bag, pulling out her brand-new waterproof phone.

"Twenty minutes till show time!" Zoe tosses her phone back into her pale blue Roxy bag. "I can't wait until the meeting!"

I squeal and pull my own thin towel out of my bag; it hadn't occurred to me that the club would provide one. I'm about to wring my hair out when at the last second I opt to dry myself off with the oversized BCC one instead. There's no reason not to take advantage of club perks while I'm here, and anyway, their towels are as soft as puppy fur.

"Way to be decisive," Zoe jokes.

"Ha ha . . . so funny." I wave my finger at her in mock annoyance. "Anyway, what do you think we'll talk about at the info session? Do you think they'll just let us work the ocean? Or do you think they'll make us guard the pool too? Do you think . . ." I stop talking for a second to flip my head upside down and towel-dry my long dirty blonde hair.

"Nervous Nelly much?" Zoe asks, peeling out of her wet suit. "If it's anything like what Zach said went on last year, then the best swimmers will be guarding the ocean with the senior guards and then everyone else will be assigned to the pool. And I heard—"

"Excuse me." A woman resembling Betty White from her *Golden Girls* days steps between Zoe and me. In one hand she balances a tray and in the other she holds a folded navy cloth. "You're Abby Berkeley, right?"

I nod.

"I'm your new boss," she replies, neglecting to mention her name. She hands the folded cloth to me and I open it to discover that it's an apron. The words *Sunset Snack Bar* are inscribed across the pocket.

"Thank you," I say, politely.

The woman smoothes out her matching apron and turns around. She opens her mouth to say something when her face lights up. "Zoe, I didn't realize that was you! It's so nice to see you again."

"Oh. I'm sorry . . ." Zoe looks at my boss's nametag, quickly reading it. "How are you . . . Lilly?"

I keep my head down and gather my things, wondering how, with so many club members, my new manager can pick Zoe out of a crowd.

"Good, sweetheart. But, more importantly, how are you? How's the family? Did your brother leave for Europe yet?" Lilly sets her tray down on the table behind our lounge chairs.

"Yup. He's gone for the entire summer." Zoe pumps her fist.

"Is he attending that basketball camp in Germany your mother was raving about?" Lilly asks, her voice dripping with sweetness.

13

"Yeah. But that's nothing compared to what *we're* doing."

"And what's that?"

"Abby and I are not *only* the club's newest lifeguards, but we're also starting our own babysitting service. You know, to help the moms who need a break or maybe want a date night."

"Really?" Lilly glances at me, her eyes wide. "I'll make sure I spread the word," she says, probably wondering how I'm going to swing it all.

"Thanks. It's my first business venture," Zoe adds.

"That's wonderful. Your mother must be so proud of you and Zach." Lilly turns back around to face me. "I didn't realize you two were friends."

I clutch the apron.

Zoe's forehead wrinkles and she gives me a crooked smile. "Yup, Abby and I have been best friends forever."

"We played softball together from the time we were six," I add, hoping the Zoe connection scores early points with my new boss.

"That's sweet." Lilly picks up her tray and balances it on her open hand.

I stare at the serving dish poised on Lilly's palm and wonder how I'm ever going to do that.

"Abigail, please meet me at the snack bar tomorrow morning so we can go over a few things," Lilly continues, her singsong voice sounding more and more forced. "I figured since you have a life-guarding meeting this afternoon, I'd give you the day off."

I stand tall and smile, concentrating on making a good impression. "Thanks for being so understanding. I really appreciate it."

"Of course." Lilly nods. Then she glances at Zoe with her

sapphire eyes. "And as always, great to see you again, Zoe. Tell your mother I said hello."

As soon as Lilly walks away, I shove the apron into my Nike bag, diverting my eyes.

But Zoe is never at a loss for words.

"Okay, Wonder Woman, how many hours are you working for her again?" Zoe asks as she and I trek past the crowded pool toward the club lobby.

"I don't know. However many she needs me." I shrug, looking for somewhere to stick my towel.

Zoe stops dead in her path and turns to face me. "So does that mean we're not expanding our babysitting service this summer?"

"Uh . . . I, uh, I meant to tell you that I might not have the time now that I'm working two . . ."

Zoe swats the air and tosses her towel in a wicker basket next to the entranceway to the locker rooms. "Whatever. I plan on babysitting my butt off since it gets me away from my crazy house."

"That sounds like a good idea. . . ." My voice trails off. "Just so you know, I really do want to babysit with you, but . . ." I ball up my towel and shoot it into the wicker basket, pausing to think about how best to phrase what I'm about to say about Zoe's beloved country club. "But working the snack bar is the only way BCC will let me lifeguard. You know, it's part of the arrangement they made with me since I'm not a member."

"Ahh! This club and its rules." Zoe shakes her head. She looks like she's about to say more when she's interrupted.

"Hey, Zoe!" A tiny woman in a yellow bikini calls out. A light pink baby sling is wrapped across her chest.

"Hi, Mrs. Johnson," Zoe answers, making googly eyes at the tiny baby.

The woman stops in front of us. "Can you watch the girls for me tomorrow so I can squeeze in an extra session with my trainer? The child care here is just so crowded on Tuesdays and you know how my girls love their one-on-one time," she says, looking overwhelmed by the sleeping child attached to her.

I open my mouth to say, "I'd love to"—even though I've never met this woman before—but then I remember my other obligations.

Zoe looks at me. Then back at the woman. "Yeah. Sure. That'd be great." She digs into her bag and hands the woman a business card.

"Thanks, sweets," she says. Relief washes over her as she looks down at the card. She waves to us, adjusts the baby on her hip, and continues her trek back toward the pool.

"Business cards?" I ask.

"I was going to surprise you today with our new cards. I ordered them before I realized how much time this snack bar thing would take up." She sighs and thrusts a card into my hand.

"Zoe, this is adorable!" I exclaim. The card is framed in a cute pastel pattern with the words *A to Z Beachwood Babysitting Service* written at the top.

"Would you expect anything less?" she asks, her eyebrows raised.

"From you? Never." I shake my head.

"You get it, right? 'A' for Abby. 'Z' for Zoe."

"I get it. We're linked, remember?" I pull my friendship necklace from my bag and show her the *A* and *Z* letter charms hanging there.

Zoe fingers the matching charm around her neck. "But now I feel like I should probably cross off the 'A' from the card. . . ."

"Don't be silly. I'll find a way—"

"Awesome," Zoe quickly interjects. "Because I really need you. The parents love you." Zoe shoves the cards into her bag, clearly relieved that I was so easy to win over.

"So, on a different note, want to tell me what that poster is for?" I point to a framed poster next to the locker room doors. It's filled with pictures of what resembles some sort of feast.

"It's for the Last Blast Luau!" Zoe exclaims.

"The what?"

"The Last Blast Luau! It's just the biggest party of the summer. Comes after the competition. They hold it every year as kind of a two-part thing."

"So, have you been?"

"No, I wasn't 'old enough.'" Zoe rolls her eyes. "I told you this club had a lot of rules. For the Luau, the rules are that you have to be at least fifteen to attend and . . ." She stops herself.

"Really?" I lean toward the poster, trying to get a better look. I notice one of the guys in the background looks a lot like Brody. I squint. Must be my imagination. Again.

When I turn around, Zoe's already deep in conversation with a familiar-looking girl dressed in a red BCC Lifeguard Y-back workout bikini. Is there anyone here who doesn't know Zoe?

"Hey, I'm Abby," I say to the girl, stepping next to Zoe. It's obvious this girl is a lifeguard—not only is she wearing the right attire, but her chiseled shoulders have the look of extensive training. I might as well get to know her.

"Yeah. Hey." She flicks her brunette hair over her shoulder, not even bothering to glance my way. "So, is your brother here?" she asks

Zoe. As she's talking, Allison and Brooke, two ultra-chic girls from B-Dub, come up behind her. They're clad in sheer sundresses over bikinis and swarm around her like the president's security detail.

"Nope." Zoe shrugs. "He's in Europe till the end of August. At basketball camp."

"Oh, that's a shame. I was looking forward to hanging with him this summer."

"You were looking to do more than hang with him, Lexi." Allison elbows her.

"Yeah, now that Kylie is a thing of the past . . ." Brooke giggles.

"And so is you-know-who . . ." Allison adds, raising her eyebrows like she knows she's saying something she shouldn't.

Lexi shoots them both a look like *shut up now, you morons*. Then she tells Zoe that she'll catch her later and with that she saunters past us. Allison and Brooke trail behind her like goslings following their mother. Allison manages to give me a small wave goodbye before being pulled back into the gaggle.

"And I thought Allison and Brooke were Violet Montgomery's girls," I say, mockingly. "They always seemed to be such loyal followers at school."

"They would follow a toddler if they thought the kid was going to be the next Justin Bieber."

I snort. "Regardless, I'd kill for that girl Lexi's shoulders."

"I know. Her parents set her up with this amazing trainer in LA who works with all the professional athletes," Zoe replies.

And that's when it hits me. "Wait. Lexi? Lexi Smalls."

"Yeah . . ."

"She was at the invitational in San Fran. I beat her by a stroke in the freestyle. And from what I heard, she kicked butt in tournaments all year long."

"Yup. That's her."

"That's right! I knew I'd seen her somewhere before. I remember Lexi's dad totally reamed her out after I beat her. He screamed so loud his voice echoed throughout the entire gym. I even felt sorry for her. Now not so much."

"It's hard to feel sorry for Lexi."

"So what's her deal? You know, besides me beating her at the invitational and her having psychotic parents?"

Zoe scales two gray stone steps and passes in front of a comfy window seat filled with plush navy cushions. "Let's just say this: Lexi Smalls makes Violet Montgomery look like a kitten."

"Seriously?"

"Lexi is like Violet but instead of using her powers for evil as an 'actress,' she uses them to be a total swimming superstar. I hear that when Lexi's done with a swim meet at school, her classmates flock to her like she's Lady Gaga."

"Wait, where does she go to school again?" I stop midstride, hoping that Zoe isn't about to say what I think she is.

"Upper Crest."

Heat fills my body. Upper Crest is the school that Brody went to. I force myself to keep calm. "Oh right, the same private school that uh . . ."—*not Brody, not Brody*—"Amber McDonald went to before she transferred to B-Dub this spring."

"Yup. That's how I got the inside deets."

"Well, maybe things will be different at the club. . . ."

"Ha! Doubt it. Since Violet and Hannah are in the South of France this summer, Lexi is definitely ready to take over Vi's reign as top dog."

"Well, hopefully our captain will put her in her place," I reply, trying to be the logical one.

"That's just it. Loco Lex *is* our captain this year." Zoe stops in front of a door emblazoned with a gold plate on which the word, *Lifeguards* is stamped.

"Who would name someone like that captain?"

Zoe grabs my arm and pulls me down the hall beside a large potted plant. She lowers her voice when a cute group of guys in red swim trunks say hi to her. They walk through the door we were just standing in front of.

"That's the thing. Captains aren't named here. They're earned through that intra-squad competition I was telling you about. They hold it at the end of the summer and whoever wins is named captain and guaranteed a college scholarship."

"Wait. What? Did you see her Prada beach bag? I can think of at least ten of my neighbors who could use a scholarship before her," I say with a sigh.

Another member brushes by us. Her Louis Vuitton purse bangs into my arm, jolting me into action. "Scratch that. Is there even a single club member who actually needs a college scholarship? Seems to me that most of the families here could endow their own."

"That's not the point." Zoe lowers her voice to a whisper. "It's a total status thing to guard here. And if you win the scholarship, not only do you earn bragging rights, but all the members make this huge deal out of you. You become BCC royalty."

I immediately begin to formulate a plan to snag the scholarship. I'm sure if I win, the club will give me "member status." But most of all, then I could guarantee myself money for college before I even begin my sophomore year of high school. And I thought I would have to pray to get noticed through one of my sports at B-Dub! My insides begin to bubble like a Jacuzzi just thinking about the scholarship.

Zoe continues. "And get this. Lexi didn't exactly win last year. She came in second place. The guy who won decided not to work at the club again, so he gave the money back and they gave the captain rank to Lexi."

"So she didn't even earn it outright?"

"Uh-huh. Rumor is, though, that Lexi didn't actually get to see the moolah. So this year, she's willing to do just about anything to prove that she's deserving of the coveted Beachwood Country Club swim scholarship. And when I say anything, I mean *anything*."

"Is the event *that* competitive?" Even with what Zoe's told me about how much people at BCC love to brag, I can't imagine that Lexi and everyone else here would be as motivated as I am. Unlike the rest of them, I *need* a scholarship. It's the only way I'll be able to attend a four-year school.

"If you thought breaking the basketball, softball, and swimming lineups at B-Dub as a freshman was tough, that's nothing compared to how all-out people go for this thing."

"Zach told you all of this?"

"Yeah. So you can imagine how tough it really is. . . ."

21

I step next to her, admiring the huge plaque honoring Last Blast winners. I run my finger down the names, recognizing some of the last names from school. I can just barely make out where last year's original winner's name was listed before being replaced by Lexi's. "And I guess a non-member has never won. . . ."

"Nope. Never. Like I said, you're the first non-member to ever lifeguard here. So it'd be pretty impossible to w—" Zoe places her hand in front of her face as if she can't believe those words just tumbled out of her mouth. "Not that I don't think you can do it."

"You better believe I can." We squeeze into the team room and I look around. Lifeguards sit on folding chairs and huddle in small groups. Everyone seems totally at ease. But I'm not going to let that stop me.

This swanky club doesn't know what's about to hit it.

# Chapter Three

**I follow Zoe to** a long table set up beneath a framed panoramic black-and-white photo of the beach thirty years earlier. A woman wearing a starched white Beachwood Country Club shirt sits behind a cardboard box filled with envelopes marked "registration."

"How are you, Zoe?" the woman asks, lowering her tortoiseshell glasses onto the bridge of her nose. She graciously smiles.

"Peachy cream, Carol. As you may have already heard, I'm a lifeguard this summer," Zoe announces, going for maximum effect.

"I did hear as a matter of fact," Carol replies, wagging her finger at Zoe. She flips through the small file and finds Zoe's manila envelope in seconds. "Please pick up your gear over there." She passes Zoe the package and points to the table next to her. On it sit rows of brand-new navy blue Beachwood Country Club gym bags.

I watch Zoe attack the table, snatching a canvas bag up in

seconds. While most girls at B-Dub wouldn't be caught dead in anything but designer clothes, Zoe and I are always suckers for sporty gear.

"And you are?" Carol looks me over like she's checking out squashed soup cans masquerading as fine art.

"Abby. Abby Berkeley," I say, clearing my throat. Two girls come up behind me and try to push their way to the front to sign in. They roll their eyes when they realize that there's a line.

Carol gives them each a small grin and then begins flipping through the monogrammed envelopes. "Hmm . . ."

*Zip.*

"Check this out!" Zoe shouts, holding up a Dri-FIT tee against her chest.

I do a little bounce, eager to snag my own bag of free duds. The girls in line barely manage to control their snickers. Obviously, this isn't as big of a moment for them as it is for me.

"Berkeley with a *B*, correct?" Carol looks up.

"Yup," I say, bewildered by the delay.

"I don't see you here." Carol continues to search through the envelopes.

My stomach drops like an anchor. "What? Wait. I have my letter."

As I begin to rustle through my bag, I hear Lexi laughing from the front row behind me. Whether it's about me or something else, I'm not sure.

"Are you positive you're a member?" Carol asks, pulling out a paper. She wrinkles her forehead as she scans the list.

"Yeah. I mean, no, I'm not a . . ." I look back behind me. By this point, the line of lifeguards—all of whom appear visibly frustrated by the holdup—has grown like a weedy vine.

"I'll grab us some seats. The room is filling up fast," Zoe says, obliviously leaving me to fend for myself.

"Abby." Carol drags her finger down the paper list. "Oh. That's right! You're the new girl who's working at the snack bar this summer. We were just talking about you this morning."

"Actually, I'm new to the club but I'm not new to the beach—"

"That's great." Carol cuts me off, pulling out a manila envelope marked NON-MEMBER in black marker. "Here you go."

"Thanks," I say, tensely smiling. I tuck the envelope under my arm and quickly scan the bags. Grabbing the first one I see, I unzip it and hastily shove my envelope inside.

When I turn around to search for Zoe, Lexi calls out, "Hey, new girl!" I pretend I don't hear her and find Zoe in the back of the room.

"Did you see this?" Zoe beams, holding out the red swimsuit. "We're official!"

Seeing the gear pulls me out of my funk. I pull a bright red lifeguard visor out of my bag and shove it on top of Zoe's air-dried hair. She stands and poses.

"Work it, girl!" I shout.

We both bust out in hysterics as Zoe begins to pretend to walk the runway.

*Tweeeeet!*

At the sound of the whistle, Zoe and I jump like we've been stung by jellyfish. A bronzed woman with a streak of zinc across her nose stands in front of the ivory wall. The combination of the CPR poster hanging behind her, her surprisingly formal attire—a gray Beachwood Country Club short-sleeved collared tee neatly tucked into red shorts—and the way that she crosses her cut arms leaves no doubt in my mind. This woman means business.

"Attention!" the woman announces from the front of the room. She lets her metal whistle drop from her mouth so that it hangs from a lanyard wrapped around her neck.

"For those who don't know me . . ." The woman glances at the back of the room where Zoe and I are seated. Some of the experienced lifeguards, including Lexi and her crew, turn around, narrowing their eyes at us so that there's no confusion about who the new kids in town are.

"Ahem . . ." the woman says, "I believe I had the floor." She taps her foot on the ground in annoyance. "As I was saying, my name is Denise Mason and I will be your supervisor this summer."

Zoe slides her chair next to mine. Leaning over, she whispers, "Denise is insane. Last year she made Allison run the beach for an hour after conditioning practice because she *heard* she was dating another lifeguard."

*Guess it's a good thing I've sworn off guys for all eternity.*

"And get this. She was just talking to the guy."

"Seriously?"

"Seriously." Zoe nods.

"If the guards don't need this job, then why put up with Denise?"

"The same reason you applied. The glory. Everyone wants to work here." Zoe nods at me sagely.

I nudge her to pay attention.

"I know most of you want to jump right into a discussion about the Last Blast Competition." Denise says, adjusting her matching BCC visor.

A couple of seasoned lifeguards let out hoots.

Denise glares at the guards. They immediately stop.

"But first we're going to go over the club rules and regs. I can tell already we're going to lose some guards this year due to bad behavior."

Zoe leans toward me again. "Here we go. . . ."

"I'm going to start off by saying, first and foremost, absolutely no relationships between lifeguards and anyone who is employed by the country club. And I hope I'm making myself clear this year. That means no hand-holding with yoga instructors. No kissing bus boys"—I'm surprised to see Lexi and her friends' eyes go wide at this one—"and most importantly, no dating your fellow lifeguards. Last year, we seemed to have some misunderstandings." Denise scans the first few rows. Her dark eyes land on Allison, who immediately turns to stare at a spot on the wall.

I say a silent prayer of thanks that I'm not her.

"Ohmigod," Zoe whispers.

"I know. Can you believe she outed Allison like that on the first day? She must be dying."

Zoe's eyes are wider than a six-lane freeway. "You're not going to believe this."

"What?" I whisper back.

"The guy. The one who actually won the competition."

"Yeah?"

"He's here."

"What?"

"Look!" Zoe points to the back of the room.

"Zo, I don't even know what he looks like and we should be paying attention to Denise."

"Look!" she practically screams.

And that's when I turn behind us.

I gasp.

His neck, I'd recognize those muscular contours anywhere. His tousled brown hair, the same hair I ran my hands through. His long strapping legs, the legs that stretched out with mine on the sand. His eyes, the emerald ones that have been imprinted in my mind for the last month.

It's him. Standing in the doorway.

*Brody.*

# Chapter Four

**Droplets of sweat roll** down my back as Denise's stern voice fades away like a distant foghorn. The only sound I hear is my heart beating inside me like a drum.

"Abs . . . Are you okay?" Zoe asks.

I slink down in my chair, pulling Zoe along with me. "Shhh . . ." I say. "He'll see you."

"Who cares if he sees me?" Zoe whispers loudly. "It's Lexi who better watch her back."

"Lexi?"

"Yeah, because of the competition. How he's the one who actually won and everything . . . Isn't that what we're talking about?"

"Zoe, that's him. That's the guy."

Zoe gives me a confused look.

"The guy from the swim meet."

Zoe's eyes widen as recognition crosses her face. "Wait just one second. Your mystery guy is Brody? Brody Wilson?"

I glance around nervously, slumping deeper into my chair. "I have to get out of here."

"What? Are you kidding me? This is the best thing to happen since, well, ever!"

"How can you say that? He's here, which means he lied to me. He told me he was going to be at Michigan by now. So either *a*, he wasn't actually recruited for swimming or *b*, he just didn't want a relationship *with me*." I shake my head. My brothers were right. Guys are dogs.

"Or maybe he just didn't know he was going to be back here, since he *did* give up the captainship and everything."

I glare at Zoe. She clearly doesn't know what she's talking about. After all, she never even told me that Brody worked at the country club in the first place. Granted, I never told her his name.

"Uh, Abby. I think he's looking at you." Zoe elbows me.

"What? No!" Without thinking, I pop up to see if Zoe's right. Only then do I realize that she was just kidding. Some of the other guards glower at me, but fortunately, I duck down again before Brody notices what's going on.

Or at least I hope I do. . . .

My breath begins to rise and fall in heaping gasps and I force myself to concentrate on what Denise is saying. "Our club members expect certain standards to be met," Denise continues, "which in turn means we expect nothing but the best from our lifeguards."

I can't help it. It doesn't take two seconds before I start tuning out Denise's droning. Again. How can all the other guards look so calm? Brody friggin' Wilson is here!

I give myself a mental slap in the face. *Get a hold of yourself, Abby Berkeley.*

"To be the best, you have to work hard." Denise faces us.

I don't know if it's because my ragged breathing is making me lightheaded, but I start to feel like Brody's staring at the back of my head.

*I can't look. I just can't.*

"Look around," Denise says.

Of course. Now he's sure to notice me.

Heads turn back and forth. Some smile and wave. Others sit relaxed back on their chairs. I cringe and chew on my nail.

"There are a combined twenty-five senior and junior guards in this room. Do the math. That's way too many. We do this on purpose."

I stare at the floor, attempting to mentally invoke long dormant powers of teleportation. It doesn't work.

"Some of you will quit because you can't hack it in the water. Others will be fired because they can't hack it on land. But know this: one bad move and you're history. No exceptions."

"Let's hope she makes one exception," Zoe whispers, raising her eyebrows in Brody's direction. "For a certain Miss Berkeley and Mr. Wilson."

I shudder. What if Denise *does* find out about my history with Brody? Would that alone be enough to disqualify me? If she can be mad at Allison a year later for something that turned out to be totally insignificant, then I can only imagine what she'd do to me if she ever discovered all the Brody-related thoughts that have been flying through my head for the past thirty days.

"Please refer to the schedule included in your packets. You will be required to condition before and after your shifts. Junior guards who are in the top five in conditioning during the first few sessions will be paired up with a senior guard to learn to work the beach. The remaining junior guards will be assigned to the pool. You will receive your assignments by the end of the week. More specific information can be found in your folders."

"Did you hear that? You and Brody will be paired up! I know it!" Zoe elbows me.

I reach down and dig into my bag before I throw up.

"Any questions?" Denise asks. She takes the room's silence as a call to continue. "If there are no questions about conditioning, then let's take a moment to go over what I know you're all anxious to hear about: the Last Blast Competition."

The guards around me instantly perk up as Denise grabs papers from the side table. "The competition will be held at the end of August just as it has been in years prior."

I pick my head up. That's what I need to distract me. The competition. I'll be so busy training to win the scholarship I won't have time for Brody.

"Just like last year, two captains will be selected on the basis of seniority. They will then have the opportunity to select their teams and choose a group name. Men and women each will compete separately in three events, earning points for their respective squads. The winning team will take home the trophy and—" she pauses for emphasis, "the leading scorer for the winning team will win a college scholarship of twenty-thousand dollars per year."

*Twenty-thousand dollars! Per year!* I set my feet on the linoleum floor like a track star ready to take off.

"I hope that everyone has been working out this spring. Conditioning begins tomorrow. Now, I'll ask you once more: Are there any questions?" Denise lets out a deep breath and hastily scans the room. "I guess not. Then, in that case, our first meeting is officially dismissed."

Before Denise can finish the *s* sound in *dismissed*, I dart out of my seat. I'm in such a hurry to escape that my bag snags on the arm of my chair. It pulls and rips, scattering the contents across the carpet.

*No! Not the apron.* I search for it, hysterical. Guards begin to gather around me. Finally, I spot the navy cloth resting against a chair leg in the distance. If I can just grab the cloth before Brody sees me, maybe I'll manage to escape with at least some of my dignity intact.

I make a last-ditch attempt to reach for the apron, hoping to feel the familiar cotton beneath my fingers.

Instead, a warm hand folds over mine.

# Chapter Five

**"Abby . . ."**

The word hangs there. But I'm too disoriented to even recognize it as my name.

"Abby?" Brody says it again, this time as a question. Like *earth to Abby*, only soft, sweet.

I look down and realize that my hand is still wrapped in his. His fingers are warm and rough, the fingers of someone who isn't afraid to get a little dirty. I like that about him. My breath catches in my throat. *What am I doing thinking about Brody Wilson's fingers?*

I pull my hand back abruptly. "Uh, uh . . . I gotta go."

"Wait," Brody reaches out to me again. This time his hand lands on my arm.

Shivers run down my spine and once again I'm momentarily paralyzed.

"I'm so glad you came."

My eyes travel to his thick lips, watching them as they form each individual syllable. For a moment, it's as if his lips are disassociated from the rest of his body. All I can think about is how amazing they would feel pressed against my own. How luscious they *did* feel pressed against my own.

"I was actually looking forward to seeing you here today."

I take a tiny step backward and am finally jolted from my daydream. "Wait, how did you know I was supposed to be here? I just found out a couple days ago."

Brody gives me a sheepish grin. "When Denise told me that a spot on the team opened up and she received an application from an Abby Berkeley"—he bends down and picks up my manila packet from the floor—"I had to step in."

"You what?" I ask, confused. I take the folder from his outstretched hand.

"I couldn't believe it was really you. What are the odds?"

"Yeah. Small world." I shove the stupid non-member packet in my bag. I glance at the doorway, still tempted to flee. Then I look back at Brody and before I know it, I'm letting everything out. "Look, I haven't seen you since you told me that you didn't want to go out with me. And now you're here when you said you were going to be in Michigan. And I'm about to start lifeguarding at this fancy club of yours and I really want to make a good impression. So just be honest with me. What's up?"

"I recommended you for the job." He pushes back his sideswept brown hair.

"You what?!"

"I advocated for you to get the lifeguarding job. And surprisingly enough, Denise listened to me." Brody looks down at me and gives me a smirk that somehow manages to convey both shame at being found out and the glee of a five-year-old child who knows he's gotten away with murder. "I'm sorry that they're also making you work at the snack bar, but I'm just glad to see you here."

I let Brody's alleged enthusiasm wash over me and then place my hands on my hips. "Are you telling me that I couldn't have gotten this job by myself?"

"Wait, no. That's not what I meant—"

I cut him off. "Because you of all people should know what an accomplished swimmer I am."

"I do, Abby—"

"I mean, you were there at the conference."

"I know, which is why—"

"Ahem," says a voice, interrupting Brody mid-sentence. The word is quickly followed by two quick taps on my shoulder. When I turn around, Lexi holds out my apron, "I'm sorry to get in the way of whatever's going on here, but I believe this is yours."

Quicker than I can say *mortified*, I snatch the apron from her grasp.

"So tell me, will you be *guarding* the snack bar this summer?" Lexi snorts.

I ball my fists.

"You've got yourself a real two-for-one here, Brody," Lexi continues, glancing his way. "You know, lifeguard by day, snack girl by night?"

My face reddens with humiliation. If she were anyone other than my captain, I'd knock her right out of her overpriced coffee-colored

Ugg flip-flops. As it is, I'm thinking of doing so when Brody steps forward.

"Lay off her, Lex," he says.

My cheeks heat up—Brody defended me! But then I stiffen just as quickly. I can handle this myself.

"Oh, don't worry about us, Bro. We're just having a little fun. Right, Abby?"

I grimace.

Lexi doesn't let that stop her. "So if I say, 'Thank goodness we have Abby to save us from drowning in a glass of water,' she'll know I'm just joking. Right, Abs?"

"That's enough, Lexi." Brody stands between us.

Lexi backs away, feigning humility. "Okay, okay. I'll let you two get back to your little secret tryst." She raises her eyebrows and turns to me. "I'll see you when I need a mocha." Then she charges out of the room, practically whipping us with her brown ponytail.

For a second, I forget that I'm standing in front of the same guy I've been thinking about, okay obsessing over, for the past month. "What's her deal?" I ask.

"She's just an insane competitor." Brody shrugs.

"So you two know each other well?" I imagine the two of them sneaking into an empty classroom at Upper Crest for a private canoodling session. The thought makes my stomach churn.

"Let's just say Lexi and I have known each other for a long time." He hesitates before telling me more. "Look, I wanted to—" A buzz interrupts us.

He reaches into his pocket and pulls out his phone. His face drops as he reads the text.

"I'm sorry to do this . . . but I've got to go," he says abruptly. Then he dashes toward the door.

*What the?* I watch him disappear, feeling as if the world has just dropped out beneath me.

And then suddenly there he is, back by my side just as quickly as he vanished. He moves in as if he's about to kiss me on the cheek, but then at the last second he squeezes my hand instead. "I'm so glad you're here."

And then he's gone. For real this time.

And I'm left totally confused.

"What was that?" Zoe appears next to me.

"I'm not exactly sure," I say, feeling like my feet are stuck in cement.

"Did he say anything about Michigan?"

"Not a thing," I stare at the empty doorway.

"That's weird. So what are you going to do?"

"I have no idea."

Zoe sniggers.

"What?" I ask, wondering what about this could possibly be funny.

"I was just thinking . . ."

"Yeah?"

"Wait until he meets your brothers."

# Chapter Six

**Four one two. Roger,** the scanner screams the next morning.

I'm flying down the Pacific Coast Highway in my dad's stuffy patrol car en route to the country club. Since I agreed to meet Lilly at the Sunset Snack Bar an hour earlier than Zoe's reporting time, I had to forego Zoe's mom's offer to drive me and beg my dad for a lift. I suspect that this won't be the last time I have to ask him to take me.

*Roger.*

My legs stick to the black leather seat as the air conditioning blows full blast, loosening blonde hairs from my high ponytail. If the Lysol scent trailing from the backseat is an indicator of whatever happened last night, it must have been a rough one.

"So tell me again why I'm driving you twenty minutes out of the way to this *ridiculous* beach club when you could have easily worked at the swim club around the corner from our house?" My dad rests one hand across the steering wheel while pressing keys on the mounted dashboard computer with the other.

"Only if you tell me why you have to drive me everywhere in this *ridiculous* police car." I sigh, watching the palm trees fly past the window. "I just love making a grand entrance everywhere I go."

*Wern. Wern. Wern. Wern.*

"Oh my God, Dad! Shut off the siren!" I scream at my dad, who's grinning like Kobe Bryant hanging from a rim. Then I slide down in my seat so no one can spot me.

He flicks the switch. "You used to love that siren."

"Maybe when I was five." I let out a sigh. "But now not so much."

"Someone is drinking the Beachwood Country Club Kool-Aid." The brim of his police hat casts a shadow over his navy eyes.

"First off, no I'm not. And in case you haven't noticed where I've been heading with my book bag every morning for the past year, I've kind of been attending B-Dub with all the same girls from the club. So it's not exactly new territory." I stretch out my legs against my new lifeguard bag resting on the floor. I'm still so relieved that my knee doesn't feel super stiff when I move it.

The scanner cuts in again and we pause. *Blue nineteen-ninety three. Suspect known. Five. Six. Forty one.*

My nervousness gets the best of me and I sit on my left leg. "But seriously, working at BCC is an opportunity of a lifetime. I wouldn't get the chance to work the beach at my age anywhere else."

Then again, I also wouldn't have had a super strange encounter with Brody anywhere else . . . but there's no need for my dad to know about that.

"Don't sit on your leg when you're in a moving vehicle." He

points to me with his right hand, totally ignoring what I just said. "If we were involved in an MVA at this speed . . . ." He points to his dashboard. "You would lose that leg."

I roll my eyes. What are the chances of a moving vehicle accident with a cop driving? I unravel my leg and bump my knee on the rifle rack.

Ouch.

"It's not like you minded when Robby was a lifeguard at the same beach," I add.

"That's entirely different. The beach was public at the time. You know as well as I do Robby was hired by the county, not by some elitist private club."

*Copy. Ten. Four.*

My father lets out a deep breath. "I just can't stand these private country clubs, especially Beachwood. Coming in and wrecking the beach environment just so these people can be pampered with restaurants and bars and saunas. What ever happened to going to the beach with a surfboard and nothing else? Just being with your friends and hanging ten. That's what I did in my day."

I let out a sigh. Here we go.

*Ten. Alpha. Zeta. Beta.*

"And then they think they own the beach because they pay tens of thousands of dollars?" my dad continues. "Don't they realize that California beaches are public? My father patrolled these beaches during World War II. They belong to all of us."

"Dad, I know you don't like BCC. But it's a nice job and my friends are all there."

He holds out his hand. "You think? It doesn't bother you how these stuck-up snobs only want certain kinds of people around them?"

I stare out the window again, fuming.

"Did you know you can't even become a member of the club unless you're sponsored by another member? It's not just good enough to have money. Oh no. You have to be one of the chosen few. Who the hell do these people think they are? I'm glad the protestors are pushing the city to do something about all of this crazy privatization. It's ridiculous."

"Uh, Dad, you're a police officer. You work the protests. You're not really supposed to have an opinion."

My dad grunts. "I just can't stand it that these people think they can buy anything for the right price. We didn't bring you up like that."

"Yeah Dad, I know. But—"

"It's great that you always try to see the best in everyone, Abby, but you'll learn that people who think they can buy whatever they want are trouble."

"Dad, it's . . ."

"Sometimes I wonder if . . . if your mother and I should have agreed to send you to Beachwood Academy in the first place."

I roll my eyes. My mother and father have questioned their decision to send me to B-Dub since the day they signed the paperwork. "These people that you're talking about are my friends. You've met Zoe. Is she like that?"

"One person doesn't change anything." My dad doesn't move his eyes from the road.

"Fine. Then think of all the amazing things I've gotten to do because I go to Beachwood, like, say, the Desert Invitational softball tournament and the gorgeous ring ceremony they held at the club in honor of our basketball championship."

My dad groans. "Yeah, that was great. They took you to the club during the school year. Seems a little incestuous to me."

"Dad, come on. How about the Colorado River retreat and being part of mock trial and the Greek Club? Robby, Alex, and Frankie didn't get to do any of that."

"Exactly. And your brothers turned out just fine." My dad glances at me suspiciously out of the corner of his eye. "Robby is a respected police officer, Alex is attending the academy, and Frankie is thinking about a career in landscape design. All publicly educated."

"I don't know, Dad. Maybe you're drinking some Kool-Aid of your own."

*California license plate. Eight. Six. Alpha. Beta. Nine. Four.*
*Roger.*

While my dad is distracted, I forge on. "The beach club is just like the academy. Just another amazing opportunity to prepare me for my future. Like, did you know that BCC offers a college scholarship to the winner of their annual intra-squad competition?"

"And let me guess, you're planning on competing?"

"Yup."

My dad squeezes the steering wheel. "What's wrong with community college? Your brothers loved their experiences at Los Angeles County College."

"What's wrong with me doing something different? I'm not my brothers, Dad." I repeat what I've said for years. "You know it's—"

*Nine. Thirteen. Pacific Coast Highway. Five. Six. One.*

"Been my dream to play a sport at a four-year school since I threw my first softball."

"There's no doubt that you're developing into a phenomenal athlete, Abby. But don't get your hopes up about that scholarship."

"Whatever." I drum my fingers on the cool glass separating the backseat from the front.

"All I'm saying is BCC is a tight-knit group. They'll probably give that scholarship to one of their own."

Zoe's words replay in my mind: *You're the first non–club member to ever man a lifeguard chair here. You should be so proud.* An image of the plaque with the winning names pops up in my head.

*Tap. Tap. Tap.* My dad's fingers fly across the keyboard. "I've done a lot of work in this county over the years, Abigail. I have a lot of experience dealing with all sorts of people."

"I already told you, Dad. My friends aren't like that." I ignore Lexi's angry face flashing before my eyes.

"I just don't want to see you end up disappointed. That's all."

The police car seems a bit stuffier than normal today. I roll down the window and breathe in the fresh salty air.

"The air is on," he says. "Taxpayer money."

"I know," I say.

"See what I mean? One year at Beachwood and you've already forgotten the value of a dollar."

My dad turns off the Pacific Coast Highway and into the entrance to the club. He pulls behind a cherry-red Porsche and a sleek silver Ferrari in the valet line. Protestors armed with *Free the Beach* and *Stop Building on Our Beach* signs surround the entrance.

I point to a protestor with long straggly hair. "Look Dad, it's Paul from down the street."

As my dad turns to face me, his leather belt squeaks. He ignores my comment about Paul. "I know you're excited about all this." He motions toward the club's imposing entranceway. "Just be careful."

"I will," I say before hesitantly climbing out.

As I walk toward the entrance, feeling like a bit of a scab, protestors yell and shake their signs.

"Beaches are gifts from God. They can't be bought!" a woman yells.

A guy in faded board shorts holds a sign that says, *I used to surf here.*

"Me too," I whisper.

Then I step in front of the club entranceway. The doorman opens the double wooden doors for me to walk through.

And I do.

# Chapter Seven

**I tie on my** stiff apron and take in the sights and sounds of the club as I walk over to the Sunset Snack Bar (surreptitiously, of course—I can't risk running into Brody and having him mess up my first official day of snack bar duty). I stare through the small opening in the ivory-and-blue tiled wall behind the counter and can just make out chefs preparing dishes—mostly yogurt and granola from the looks of it—for their early morning clientele.

Directly in front of me, I see Lilly talking to a woman seated on a stool. The woman stares at a chalkboard menu hung above the kitchen window. She's dressed in a white flowing skirt, bathing suit top, and strappy leather sandals. Her black hair is cropped into a short, straight bob.

That *seems* pretty normal. . . . I don't see what my dad was talking about, saying that things here are so different from the way they are at our local swim club. Sure, the food is a teensy bit nicer, but that's not a big deal.

When Lilly sees me, she nods ever so slightly without breaking her conversation. She doesn't speak to me directly until the woman tells her that she needs a second to decide on her order.

"Good morning, uh . . ." she says to me, straightening up some printed menus. She looks at me searchingly, as if she knows that she's supposed to remember my name but she still can't come up with it.

"I'm Abby," I say. "Abby Berkeley . . ." My voice heightens toward the end of that last part, so that it sounds more like a question than a statement. "Zoe's friend . . ." I fiddle with the bottom of my starched apron.

"Right, of course." She smiles tightly. "You can put your bag there." She points to an open spot underneath the counter.

"Thanks so much for allowing me this opportunity," I say, shoving my lifeguard bag in the space she indicated. I search for something to say. "I really appreciate your delaying my start date so that I could concentrate on my lifeguard orientation."

Lilly takes out a cloth from the front of her apron and wipes down the marble counter. "Of course. Now the easiest way for me to train you is for you to just watch what I do. If you have any questions, don't hesitate to stop me. Sound good?" Lilly doesn't wait for my response.

I stiffen, wondering if this is what the entire summer will be like, when I catch sight of a guy manning the bar adjacent to our counter. He's dressed in a navy collared shirt with "BCC" embroidered on his left breast pocket. His eyes meet mine and I give him a little wave. He smirks and I realize how silly I must look, standing there in my apron with what I'm sure is a confused expression on my face. I quickly look away and force myself to pay attention to Lilly. "How long have you been working here?" I ask her.

"Since it opened," she says, ferociously rubbing a towel over what appears to be an oil stain on one of the stool cushions.

"Wow. That must have been a long time, probably right when I stopped coming to the beach as a kid." I expect her to ask why I stopped coming, but the question doesn't seem to cross her mind.

Confused, I locate a towel of my own and attempt to help her with the cleaning, but she shakes her head, affirming that my help isn't necessary.

"Who worked the snack bar last year?" I ask, desperate to keep the conversation going.

"Oh." Lilly stops cleaning, seemingly resigning herself to the reality of the stain. She pushes her glasses up the bridge of her nose. "Jason did." She glances at the guy who I'd been eyeing just moments ago. "He's been with us for a few years now. But there was another girl too. Hmm . . . her name escapes me." Lilly taps her chin with her finger. "Was it Ann? Jennifer? I can't remember."

I imagine what my dad would say to that. Probably something like, "See, I told you that people like us don't matter to them." But then I push the thought out of my mind just as quickly as it came. Lilly works the snack bar. She *is* someone like us. Whatever that means.

"Excuse me. What do you think of the asparagus and goat

cheese *omelette*?" The woman seated at the stool interrupts us, tucking a poker-straight chunk of hair behind her ear.

"It's divine, Stacey," Lilly answers, her monotone voice replaced with a peppy professional pitch.

"Then, the *omelette* it is . . ." Stacey says, dragging out her voice like she's moaning. She says the word *omelette* with a French accent.

I watch Lilly relay the order to two guys with gleaming white chef hats. Clangs, sizzles, and pops immediately follow.

"Could you add a mimosa to that too?" Stacey asks, waving over the bartender who Lilly'd previously identified as Jason.

"Sure!" he says, pretending to tip an imaginary hat toward her. "It'll just be one moment." I watch him as he assembles the ingredients with the practiced ease of a pro. First, he pours in some champagne. Then some orange juice. The drink fizzes. It looks like he's about to hand the glass over to Stacey when all of a sudden he thinks better of it. He grabs a bottle of hot sauce from a nearby condiment tray and, glancing definitively in my direction, mimes as if he's about to pour a few drops in.

My stomach drops and I wave both arms around like a maniac, mouthing, "Don't do it!" I flip back to Stacey before I can see whether Jason has listened to me, scared that she saw what he was about to do. Fortunately, she's pulled out an iPad, seemingly out of thin air, and appears to be reading. Lilly, meanwhile, is conversing with one of the chefs. I turn back to Jason. He's placed a white napkin in front of Stacey. He sets the drink down, grinning at me as he does so.

I look at the drink, frantic. Then I search for the bottle of hot sauce with my eyes. I find it back on the condiment tray, unopened.

*Phew.*

Jason winks at me as he returns to his spot at the bar. Mr. Murphy, Zoe's dad, has appeared at the bar stool in front of him. He nods at me in recognition and takes out his BlackBerry.

*Ding,* he rings the service bell. *Ding. Ding.* Clearly, he's impatient.

"A little help, please," says a voice. I turn around to find Lilly standing there with a dish balanced on each hand. Her eyes narrow, making her seem more like the evil hag from *Snow White* than a graduate of *The Golden Girls*.

"Sorry about that," I say in a rush.

I grab the plates from her, even though she'd previously told me just to observe, and take them to the only table that's not yet been served. I say a silent prayer of thanks that only a handful of tables are occupied. It's still a bit early for people to be dining.

I place the plates down and am surprised to discover two girls who can't be more than ten staring up at me. Now the orders—one French toast and one chocolate chip pancakes—make more sense. The girls are dressed in Lilly Pulitzer sundresses and are drinking iced tea. If I'd glanced at them quickly, I would have definitely pegged them for thirty-something ladies who lunch.

"Thank you," one of them mouths before sticking a giant bite of French toast in her mouth. She struggles to swallow it, getting syrup on her face and in her bright red hair.

Now she looks more like a nine-year old.

Her friend's eyes widen in horror. She strains to regain their collective composure. "Could you put this on our account please?" she asks, flipping her blonde hair.

"Uh, okay," I stammer.

I walk back to find Jason shaking his head.

"Those girls asked if their order could be placed on their account," I say to Lilly.

"Okay," she replies without inflection. I can't tell if the look on her face is expectant or ambivalent.

I rush to fill the silence, worried that I may have already made a mistake. "But they didn't give me a card or anything."

"Yes, that's fine," says Lilly, ringing up what appears to be Stacey's order.

"So . . . um, how do the members pay?"

Lilly looks at me directly. "You really have a lot of questions, don't you?" Once again Lilly doesn't wait for my response. "Every member has an account number. You look up their name in the system and charge it to their account. That way we don't have to bother the members with trivial things like exchanging money or credit cards."

I stop myself from asking, *On what planet is money trivial?* Instead, I ask, "So what if I don't know the members' names?"

"You will," Lilly replies with a shrug.

"Ahem, a little help please," Stacey calls out, using the exact same phrasing and tone that Lilly just used with me. She places her iPad inside an Hermès canvas beach bag while balancing her omelet and mimosa. "I'm heading to my cabana."

"Of course, of course," Lilly answers, rushing around the counter. "I wish you'd asked before you went through the trouble of packing everything up."

"I know, I know. My husband always tells me that I need to stop trying to do everything myself."

Lilly smiles and I don't know whether it's because I've now spent a few minutes with the woman or because of what Stacey just said, but this time the gesture seems to be without a hint of sincerity.

"Uh, wait!" I call out to her.

"Yes?" Lilly turns to me, her eyes narrowing even further.

"What should I do while you're gone?" I ask.

Lilly's nostrils flare. "You'll be okay. It's still early. The snack bar won't get crowded for another hour. And besides"—Lilly eyes me up and down as if assessing if I'm worthy—"you'll be here without me a lot this summer."

I swallow a lump in my throat. *Great.* Even when I worked the local ice cream stand, they trained me for a week before they let me serve without supervision.

I look around the snack bar, attempting to figure out what to do next. I take in the aromas coming from the kitchen and glance down at the glass cabinets to admire the desserts on display—strawberry yogurt parfait, sorbet, gelato, apple torte, cupcake trio. My admiration gets a little out of hand, though, and it's not long before I'm so consumed with imagining how delicious the desserts would taste that when Jason calls out, "Hey!" I jump back in surprise. I place my hand over my chest to slow my racing heart.

"Didn't mean to freak you out." Jason says, showing off his dimples as he smiles. He's made his way to my side of the counter.

"Sorry . . . I'm a little jumpy today." I tuck my hands into my apron pocket. Feeling awkward, I pull them out, opting to place them on top of the bar instead.

"Hi," he says. "I'm Jason." He grabs a can of soda from the fridge and cracks it open.

"I know who you are," I reply.

"Are you sure? Because you're acting like you're afraid I might pounce." He does a little hyena impression.

"Yeah, well, you caught me off guard. A few t—uh . . ." I'm distracted by Jason's motioning to the soda.

"Want one?" he asks.

"Are you planning on paying for it?"

"Nah, I don't really pay for things here. Figure it's not hurting anyone."

I think back to the little girls who told me to put their breakfasts on their accounts. Their *parents'* accounts, I now realize. "No thanks." I shrug.

"Okay, sorry Miss I-Don't-Break-the-Rules."

"Don't call me that. You don't know anything about me. For all you know, I might just not be thirsty right now."

"Okay, I'm sorry. You're right. I don't know anything about you. I don't even know your name. Let's start from the beginning. And let's do it right this time. I'm Jason and you are?" Jason puts out his hand.

"Abby."

"Nice to meet you Abby," he says, shaking my hand. "And do you have a last name?"

"Berkeley."

"Ooh, like the college. I hope you're not one of *those* girls."

"Those girls?" I ask, watching him stop to take a swig of soda.

"Girls who have their names on the sides of university buildings."

"Do you think one of *those* girls would be working the snack bar?" I place my hands on my hips and look around—hopefully casually—to see if there's anything that needs doing. I would hate to have Lilly come back to find that I let my duties slip my first day on the job.

"I was just checking. But fair point." Jason pauses, trying to see what I'm looking at. When he realizes that I'm just casing the joint, he turns back to his own section. Mr. Murphy is still sitting there in his crumpled suit, his BlackBerry now forgotten on the counter, but other than that, Jason has no other customers. He takes that as his cue to continue our conversation. "So, Abby Berkeley, what's your story?"

"My story?"

"Yeah, how'd you end up at the Sunset Snack Bar?"

"It's a condition of my being a lifeguard here. Since I'm not a member."

"Aha! That explains it."

"That explains what?"

"That explains why you walked in with a lifeguard bag, but you're working at the snack bar. Members would never stoop to serving people their waffle fries and a Coke, and non-members aren't allowed to guard here."

"Does everyone know about that stupid rule?"

Jason laughs to himself. "I'm told that nothing stays a secret for long at the Beachwood Country Club."

"You're told?"

"Some people are more concerned with secrets here than others. Me, I don't really pay attention."

"That must be liberating."

Jason chuckles, this time more genuinely. "You know, you're funny, Abby Berkeley."

"I try."

"So you must be a really good swimmer for the higher-ups to have bent the rule."

"Yeah, I guess." Yesterday morning I would have agreed with Jason outright. But after hearing how Brody vouched for me, I'm not so sure. "But I don't think I'm the world's greatest snack girl."

"What gave you that idea?"

"One, I'm standing here talking to you instead of working—and it's only my first day. And two, Lilly didn't really seem to like me."

"Lilly doesn't like anyone."

"She seemed to like my best friend Zoe just fine."

"Did she now? And is your best friend Zoe a club member?"

"Yeah . . ." I look over at her dad. He seems to be wobbling a bit on his chair.

"Well, does that tell you anything?"

"Cynical much?"

"I just call it like I see it."

"So where are you from that you learned to be so candid?"

"Glendale," he says. "I'm going to be a junior at UCLA."

"Nice," I say. "And how did you come to work here during the summer?"

"Well, my buddy from school hooked me up with the snack bar job two years ago. And I actually wasn't planning on coming back here until I got the official upgrade from snack bar attendant to bartender." He sarcastically pumps his fist. Then he looks over his shoulder and leans closer to me. "It's not the bar in the lobby, but I'll still bring home some pretty good tips."

"I bet," I say, glancing at the two girls from earlier as they get up from their table. "So how did you snag the promotion?"

"Actually, I'm kind of shocked that they gave me the job. Bartending positions are usually saved for the club's own just in case some delinquent kid wants to work to pass the time." He shrugs.

"Really?" I wonder what my dad would say to that.

"You're still new to all this. . . . You'll see."

"So . . . uh, what is college like?" I ask. I've had enough Beachwood bashing for one day.

"College is a blast." Jason smirks, giving off a devilish grin.

After a few seconds of awkward silence, I look down at the bar and count the navy granite swirls.

"I really shouldn't complain. It's actually a good gig to work at the club," Jason says, probably more for my benefit than his.

I look up, deciding to take him at his word. "I feel so lucky to have landed the job. It's such a great opportunity, especially because it allows me to participate in the Last Blast scholarship competition at the end of the summer. And I . . ."

"Whoa. Slow down there, Employee of the Month." Jason peeks over his shoulder. "That's a lot of enthusiasm for the snack bar."

"Well . . . I . . ." My face flushes. "I'm just excited to be working here on the beach with my friends. Last summer, I worked at an ice cream parlor down the street from my house." I lean over the counter to stress the most important detail: "An ice cream parlor that had no air conditioning."

"And you're going to wish you were back there, sweating your butt off, by the end of this summer." Jason drums his knuckles on the counter.

I begin to nervously straighten the seashell salt and pepper shakers. "What do you mean?"

"I don't want to freak you out, but you know, the members here are a little different . . ." He pauses and looks around again. "From you and me, that is."

"You sound like my dad. But so far it's good. I mean, my friends love it here."

"Of course they do. They're members." Jason stands up from the stool. "I just hope you have thick skin."

"I go to school with a whole bunch of the same girls. Sure, they can be a little over the top sometimes, but really, it's—"

"You'll see," Jason says, cutting me off. He walks over to Zoe's father, helping him out of his stool and handing him his BlackBerry. They head inside to the club lobby.

*Ugh,* I think. *I hope Zoe doesn't run into her father in his condition.*

I clean up the empty plates the two girls left behind and am filled with rage as I head back to the dishwasher. I don't care what Jason says. Or that my father would agree with him. Or even that Brody had a hand in my being here. There's a lifeguarding competition to be won, and I will not stoop to their level.

# Chapter Eight

**"Abby!"** Kylie Collins, my teammate from school, shouts as I'm recovering from my convo with Jason.

Behind her, Missy, Kylie's best friend and fellow senior, sashays toward me.

Zoe trails close behind, looking mortified. Next to her are Taylor and Amber, my basketball and softball teammates, respectively, who seem to have come for moral support. They never talked much at school, so I guess life at the club has made them fast friends.

When Kylie reaches the snack bar, she drops her caramel Frappuccino and practically lunges across the counter. "I want all the deets," she says, grabbing the top of my apron.

"Zoe Murphy, you have a big mouth," I say to my best friend as she trudges over.

Brody must seriously be the prince of this place. This is the first time that Kylie's shown any actual interest in my life other than as simply her boyfriend's sister's best friend. I try to tell Zoe as much with my mind waves, but I'm not sure the message really makes it over.

Missy shoves in front of her, almost knocking over Kylie's half-finished drink. Her bleached blonde hair is piled high in a loose bun. "So, did you and Brody do the nasty yet?"

"That boy is soooo cute . . ." Taylor whispers conspiratorially to Amber.

"I heard that," I grunt in their general direction.

Amber chimes in. "He's really such a sweetie." She climbs onto a stool next to Missy.

"Abby already knows how sweet Brody is. From what Zoe tells me, she already jumped his bones a month ago." Kylie elbows Zoe.

"You did not," I monotone to Zoe.

"Not quite—"

Kylie interrupts her. "Oh, come on. Don't be so modest," she says to me.

"Yeah, we heard about how he gave you the kiss to end all kisses." Missy winks.

Taylor and Amber giggle.

At this point, all four of them are sitting on stools, so it's easy to give them all a single brush-off. "Let me set the record straight. Yes, Brody and I kissed. Yes, it was wonderful. No, I did not know that he belonged to the club. No, I'm not dating him now. And no, I do not plan on dating him in the future."

The four of them burst out laughing. Taylor places her hand over her mouth to try to shield me from the hysterics. Zoe looks guilty, but that doesn't stop her laughter from coming on just as strong. Missy and Kylie, meanwhile, practically double over.

"And don't you dare start spreading rumors about me at this club!" I add. The last thing I need is for my brief romantic episode—one of a whopping two in my life, if you count Nick—to get back to Denise.

"Okay, okay, we get it," Kylie says. "Our lips are sealed. But let's just say that we won't be surprised if you come to think otherwise by the end of the summer."

The other girls nod sagely.

"Ugh," I exclaim. Then I turn to Amber. "I didn't expect to see you here. I thought you usually spend your summers traveling with your Amateur Softball Association team."

"On a break from ASA today. Tournament this weekend." Amber elbows Kylie. "Right, Ky?"

Kylie surprises me by grinning widely, as if her greatest dream in life was to be a utility player on the team for which Amber was pitching. "Yup. I'm playing second for Amber's team this summer." Kylie's move from pitcher to second base was a whole big to-do this past season. And it was only made possible by yours truly getting injured.

"But I'm here now!" Kylie adds, interrupting my train of thought. She moves her Dolce & Gabbana sunglasses to the top of her head.

"I still can't believe your dad let you keep your membership," Missy says to Kylie. "Isn't that what all those people outside are protesting? How the club is, like, a nature killer or something?"

The girls' eyes fix on me as if they expect the token scholarship student to have the answer. "Yeah," I stammer. "That's part of it."

"Huh," says Taylor. "So, Kylie, how'd you convince him?" She swivels in her stool, trying to find a place for her long legs.

"Don't get too excited. It's only for this year." Kylie rolls her eyes. "My dad hates the club." Apparently, Kylie and I actually have something in common. "The membership was just his way of apologizing for making me live in the Murphy's guesthouse for all those months."

"Well, now that you're here, can I interest you in any of our fine delicacies?" I motion to the dessert cabinet as if I'm Vanna White.

"I'll have a cupcake, please," Zoe pipes up.

"Coming right up!" I say overenthusiastically. I make a big production out of how I'm the greatest snack bar attendant of all time until I realize I have no idea how to open the glass case. First I try to slide it open. That doesn't work. Then I attempt to wiggle it. That doesn't work either.

"Let me try," Zoe jumps off the stool—her legs are too short to reach the ground—and walks around to meet me at the back of the counter. She attempts to open the case.

Nothing.

"It's tricky." A hand reaches around us. Jason unhooks the latch at the bottom and slides it open. When I look up to say thanks, he's already walking back to the bar.

Kylie eyes Jason like he's Robert Pattinson come to whisk her away to Forks. "Is that the guy who worked at the snack bar last year?" she asks, pointing. "He's hot!"

My friends watch Jason as he hangs sparkling stemmed glasses over the bar while chatting with an older guy in swim trunks and a tank top who's just stopped by.

"Yeah. He's the bartender now."

"Obviously," Kylie says.

"Is he a college boy?" Taylor asks.

"Yeah, UCLA." I reach inside the glass case and pull out Zoe's favorite—a vanilla cupcake with white frosting.

"Oooh, good school. I've been searching for someone to keep me busy this summer," Missy says, licking her lips.

Kylie elbows her. "I call the bartender." I find myself wondering if Kylie cares that Jason attends what used to be her dream school.

"He's mine. That boy is a two-for," Missy adds, twirling a piece of bright blonde hair around her index finger.

"A two-for?" I ask, my voice high-pitched. I cringe thinking about how Lexi called me the very same name just yesterday.

"He's hot and he can get me drinks." Missy clicks her tongue.

My skin crawls as I set up Zoe's cupcake on a napkin. No one notices.

"Love it when a guy is good for something." Kylie raises her eyebrows. She points to Zoe's cupcake. "Abs, can you also throw one my way?"

"And what about Andrew?" Taylor asks, ever the voice of reason. "Weren't you guys seeing each other?"

Missy flicks her wrist like she's shooing a fly. "Andrew. Schmandrew. It's summer. And I like to keep my options open."

I lower my voice to a whisper. "Before you two fight over Jason, I don't know if he was just having an off day today, but he seems like he's kind of a downer."

"Then he's definitely Kylie's," Amber adds. As soon as the words are out of her mouth, she looks shocked that she said them. I don't know how it happened, but Amber is clearly feeling more comfortable around Kylie than she used to.

I brace for Kylie's reaction—which I expect to come with the fury of a tornado—but then Missy cuts in, grinning mischievously. "Oh yeah, Kylie loves jerks. Her ex-boyfriend was their unofficial king."

With that, the situation—if there ever was one—diffuses immediately. Kylie tosses a balled-up napkin at Missy and the girls giggle. Then Kylie turns her attention to Zoe. "Sorry Zo," she says, reaching out to her. The jerk in question is, of course, Zach, Zoe's older brother.

"No worries. I know he can be pretty awful." Zoe shudders, then attempts to play it off. "Why do you think I'm drowning my family sorrows in a cupcake?" She takes a giant bite. "Speaking of which," she says, "I thought Kylie asked for one too. . . . Let's get some cupcakes for everyone!"

I lean back into the case, a little peeved that my best friend managed to turn her being pitied into me looking like the help. That's when I hear the sound of little feet approaching.

"Zoe!" A little girl in pink Nike shorts and matching Crocs runs toward us. She hugs Zoe's waist. "I missed you."

Zoe slides off the chair and squats down to the girl's view. "Hey, Christina Medina Flipeena. Did Mommy tell you that I'm watching you tonight?"

Christina jumps up and down. "Wanna practice my letters on my iPad with me? Please! Please! Please!"

"Sure thing, bada bing," Zoe says.

"Yes!" The little girl pumps her fist.

She darts toward her mother, the woman who'd asked Zoe to babysit yesterday. This time the woman is followed closely by a nanny pushing a stroller. Still, she seems frazzled by the bouncing child in front of her. She barely manages to wave at Zoe before the group of them shuffles off.

Zoe slides back on the stool and looks at me. "You're coming with me, right?"

"What?" I ask, confused.

"To babysitting? I figured we'd go together after what you said about how we're linked and everything."

I jut out my lip. "Sorry, Zoe. I didn't realize. I . . ."

Zoe lets out a loud sigh. "Ditching me for Brody already."

"Nah, no, no . . ." I stammer. "That's not how it is. It's just that I didn't know you wanted me to come, and I figured I'd squeeze in some extra training. You know, make sure I get top scores in conditioning so that Denise picks me for the beach? And maybe even starts to think of me as a real contender for the scholarship?"

Kylie interjects. "Ladies, ladies. Don't forget why we came." Turning to the group, she says, "How are we going to help little ole Abby here with big boy Brody?"

I feel my cheeks redden as I attempt to distract myself by entering their orders into the computer. This can't be too hard. M-U-R-P. Sure enough, Zoe's family account pops up on the screen.

Now, when Lilly returns—whenever that is—she'll at least see that I've run up a few orders.

Unfortunately, my focusing on snack bar–related tasks does nothing to stop my friends' onslaught of questions.

"Zoe said you weren't exactly psyched to see Brody yesterday," Missy says. "*Pourquoi, ma petite Abby*?"

"Abby was so caught off guard she looked like she'd seen a shark." Zoe cuts me off, wiping her mouth with a napkin. "She even caught her bag on her chair as she was leaving."

*Okay, now that was a little mean.* I ignore my friends and press a button like I saw Lilly do earlier. Except I must do something wrong because instead of the computer showing that Zoe ordered one cupcake, the charge comes up for three. I push the delete button.

"Anyway, after thinking about your dilemma . . ." Kylie continues where Missy and Zoe left off. "My advice is that you grab your boy Brody and give him a giant smacker on the lips. Then sort the details out later."

"Are you saying that he's boyfriend material, Ky?" Taylor asks, her nose buried in her cupcake.

Kylie rolls up the sleeves of her gray Eastern Connecticut softball tee. "I'm saying that he's seriously one of the nicest, cutest boys I've ever met."

"No wonder you never dated him," Missy says, smirking.

Kylie playfully elbows Missy. "You can lay off the jerk jokes now. Zachary and I are over."

"That's never stopped you before," Missy adds under her breath.

"Ouch, low blow," Zoe chimes in, her attitude masking what I recognize to be a pained expression. I'm one of the only people who knows that she still feels weird about how Kylie and Zach's relationship ended.

Kylie shakes her head like it's not a big deal. "That's true, but this time he's thousands of miles away. Plus, there's always that bartender that Missy claims she has dibs on. Or even better, Brett Davidson."

"You would give Brett Davidson another chance after he just rolled over and played dead when Zach threatened him so that he wouldn't go to the prom with you?" Zoe asks, her eyes wide with shock.

"Depends how hot he looks this summer," Kylie jibes. Then she stares directly at me. "So what's stopping you from jumping back on the Brody Wilson love train?"

I shrug. "I'm not really sure Brody's my type." I look at Amber. "Did you know him at your old school?"

"Who didn't know Brody? He's like the most popular guy at Upper Crest," Amber says, her expression earnest. "Kylie is right. He's a real sweetheart."

Zoe eggs her on. "And an amazing athlete."

"Perfect for Abby!" Taylor shouts in excitement. Then she takes one look at me and curls into a ball—her commentary isn't exactly welcome.

"Thanks so much for all of your thoughts, but what none of you have bothered to think about is, why is he here?" I bang my fist on the counter, drawing the attention of the few customers who aren't my friends.

Jason looks over at me, amused.

I notice that a pair of execs who are clearly playing hooky from work have sat down. Guess Mr. Murphy isn't the only one.

I look from them back to my friends. I don't know how I'm going to handle serving them and dealing with Kylie and co. at the same time. There's only one answer. . . .

"Sorry, can you take their order?" I ask Jason.

He winks at me, which I gather means yes, and then walks past, whispering in my ear, "You really *are* the world's worst snack bar girl." Then he makes his way to the table.

"Oooh . . ." whispers Missy. "It seems our girl Abby has two hotties on her tail. Guess Kylie and I won't be getting with Mr. Bar Man after all." Missy raises her eyebrows in Kylie's direction.

"Okay, now you're just making stuff up." I wag my finger.

Zoe comes to my aid. "Abby's right. We need to get back to the point."

I look at my best friend, relieved, and mouth, "Thank you."

"Brody," Zoe continues, her eyes flashing.

Some best friend.

Kylie tosses her cup in the nearest wastebasket. "Good call, Zo." She turns to me. "Abby. You have to find out why Mr. Wilson is back. If not for you, then at least for the rest of us."

"Really, I need to concentrate on the competition. I don't have the time."

"Wait, wait . . ." Amber looks like she's about to hyperventilate. "You don't have the time for Brody"—her eyes widen with the magnitude of her epiphany—"when maybe he gave up college to be with you?"

*Wait, what?*

"Oh. My. God." Taylor's mouth drops open.

"What exactly happened at this meet?" Kylie screeches, leaning over even further this time.

"I don't know. One minute, we met at this buffet dinner. And the next thing I knew, we were on the hotel beach, hanging out and talking. And then, it was like four o'clock in the morning."

"That's what they all say." Kylie laughs.

"You *did* mention a kiss, my chiquita banana. What are we talking here? Did you tongue wrestle?" Missy asks, always one to get right to the point.

"Hells yeah!" Zoe says, balling up her napkin.

"We didn't *really* tongue wrestle. We just kind of . . ."

"Did you like it?" Missy asks.

"I . . . uh." I pretend to look for something underneath the snack bar just as Jason returns from helping me with the order. He shakes his head when he sees me. If that slight move of his head could talk, it would say, *She's hopeless.*

This time my friends ignore him. "Then, what's the problem?" Missy rolls her eyes.

I pop back up.

"You know Abby. She doesn't trust him," Zoe adds with a look that suggests she's impressed with her own insightfulness. "It's being around all those cops all the time."

I can't believe she just said that.

"Oh wait, I know what it is," Kylie calls out. "You feel like he dumped you before his freshman year. But let me remind you—you weren't really dating."

"Kylie!" Zoe chastises her.

"I'm not saying it doesn't hurt just as much," Kylie replies. "But it's just something that people do—break up before college, make sure that they're single."

"Oh, yeah, that's just a rite of passage. Everyone does it," Missy says.

"Remember when Tamika and Derek broke up during basketball

season because they were getting ready to go to college?" Taylor contributes.

"Yeah, but yesterday Brody acted like nothing happened." I leave out the part about him getting me the job. "He even squeezed my hand."

"That's not all he wants to squeeze," Missy adds, winking at me.

Kylie lets out a sigh. "Then find out why he's not at college."

"Maybe I can find out something for Abby," Amber volunteers. "Like I said, Brody and I knew each other from school."

"Thanks, Amber. But I really don't know why we're wasting our time talking about this. Lifeguards aren't allowed to date BCC employees. Plain and simple. So it's not like we can swim off into the sunset or anything," I add.

"Hello? Why are we even debating this?" Kylie interjects. "Find out what's up and then sneak around with Brody this summer. Who cares about some stupid rule?"

"My thoughts exactly," Missy concurs.

I look at Zoe, who's nervously picking at her nails. I'm desperate for her to do the best friend thing, to get what I'm going through when no one else does. Miraculously, she rises to the occasion. "You guys don't understand. . . . If Abby breaks that rule . . . then she's gone. For good."

# Chapter Nine

**"Excuse me!"** a painfully familiar shrill voice calls out. Lexi shoves in front of Taylor, who's just about to finish off her last bite of cupcake. She's wearing a teeny red string bikini that I'm fairly sure isn't regulation. "Am I going to have to report you, Abby Berkeley? First, I catch you chatting with Brody Wilson and then I find you serving your pals from school, rather than paying customers like me."

"We're going to pay," Amber announces.

"Oh, Big Red, I almost didn't see you there. Aren't you supposed to be handcuffed to the pitching cage?"

"They let me out."

"I get it. I get it," Lexi continues. "It's always good to give the animals a chance to experience life in the wild."

Kylie glares at Lexi. "You would know."

Lexi ignores her, flipping her chestnut ponytail. Her cronies,

Allison and Brooke, file behind her, stifling barely contained giggles. Brooke waves at Missy and Kylie.

Missy's lip curls as if to say, *Don't even pretend to be my friend if you're hanging out with that.* She flounces her hair and turns her back to the intruders.

Lexi turns to me. "Nice to see you in your element."

"Stop being such a brat, Lexi," Kylie shoots back.

"Takes one to know one." Lexi cackles and playfully bumps into Kylie. Or at least she pretends to be playful about it.

"You got that right," Missy snaps her fingers at Lexi.

"Look at the hot new BCC bartender," Allison yells over to Jason. "Congrats on your new position. Got any drinks for us?"

"Ally . . ." Lexi says through gritted teeth. She shoots her girl a look that would freeze the Pacific Ocean.

Jason, meanwhile, stares at Lexi. He seems less bemused and more outright irritated now that it's not just me and my friends. I shouldn't be surprised. Lexi must be the one who gave Jason a bad impression of all club members.

Lexi's expression goes blank as soon as she notices Jason eyeing her.

It doesn't last for more than a second, though, because Amber's phone buzzes, interrupting whatever's going on. "Catch ya later, girlies," she announces. "Dad just texted me. Pitching time." Turning to Lexi, she adds, "And no, that does not make me a caged animal. That makes me the best in the state."

Lexi doesn't really listen to that second part though. Amber's mention of her dad causes Lexi to immediately glance at her phone.

Her face tenses, then relaxes when she drags her thumb across her screen.

"I'll come too," Taylor yells out. "Might as well shoot some hoops." She trails after Amber. Zoe bounces in her stool, about to announce her departure as well, but glancing at me, she decides to stay put.

"Look who it is," Jason calls from the bar.

Lexi freezes and turns his way.

*Jeez, she really thinks everything is about her.*

"Hey, baby," Jason purrs. We all look his way to find that he's talking to a platinum-blonde club member. She must be at least thirty-five, but she has curves in all the right places and her hair has the bouncing brilliance of a *Baywatch* cast member. She leans into him, loving the flirtation.

That boy must make a ton of tip money.

Lexi adjusts her bathing suit top and attempts to draw the attention back to her. "Let's see. I'll have a . . ." She scans the menu above our heads. Then she stops and fixes on me. "It must be hard working all the time. I bet that's why they normally don't let the help lifeguard. You'll probably miss out on a lot of training opportunities," she says in a saccharine sweet tone. "I hope it doesn't hurt your shot at the competition. Not that you could enter anyway since you're so busy." She snickers despite herself.

"Don't worry about me. I'll be there," I say, glaring at her.

"That's the spirit!" she exclaims.

"I'll be there to beat you like I already did during the invitational," I add, grumbling. It's a lame thing to say, but her fake enthusiasm makes me want to throw up.

"We'll see about that," Lexi replies. Then she turns back to the menu. "So, anyway, I'll have a fruit salad."

She pauses as I scribble her order on the pad of paper Lilly left out on the table.

"No. Wait. Make that a quiche lorraine."

I cross out the side salad and write *quiche lorraine*.

"Never mind, I'm not quite feeling the quiche lorraine. Too heavy. Make that a chocolate croissant."

I stop writing and stare at her.

"Are you sure?" I ask, as sweet as I can muster.

"Tsk. Tsk. You know how the club frowns upon poor service. Girls, chocolate croissants for the two of you?"

Brooke and Allison nod. I've never seen the two of them so put in their place. And only by a single look! Allison in particular looks like she's afraid to move.

"Make that three chocolate croissants," Lexi says. "On me."

"Coming right up," I say, plastering a big smile on my face. There's no way I'm letting Lexi Smalls find fault with anything about me—even if it's something as dumb as my serving abilities.

I remove the croissants from the dessert tray, place them each onto a small plate, and slide them toward Lexi and her friends. "Three chocolate croissants," I announce. I turn to the computer, knowing that if I can just manage to type in Lexi's order correctly, I'll be free of her until the next group practice. I'm very careful as I type in her last name and the items. But still, somehow I charge her for four instead of three.

*Urgh.* I rush to correct the order before anyone notices.

Just as Lexi and co. are about to leave, Kylie calls out, "Don't go. We'll miss you guys." My friends burst into giggles.

"Enjoy!" Missy yells sarcastically.

Again, my buds break out in hysterics.

"What's her beef with you two?" I ask Missy and Kylie.

"Lexi's still bent about last year," Missy says, checking her reflection in her cell phone screen.

"What happened?"

Kylie looks at Missy. "Well, we may have gotten her closest friend here fired."

"You what!?" I exclaim.

"Not really," Missy clarifies. "We just made sure that she wasn't asked back as a lifeguard."

"That's how you got your spot here, you know," Kylie adds.

*Sheesh. Does everyone here think they got me my job?*

"Huh?" Zoe says.

Missy continues, waving her hand to say that all will be clear in a moment. "Lexi's friend followed Zach around while they were both guarding last summer. We don't know whether anything *actually* happened between them, but Zach flirted with her like he does everyone with girl parts—"

"Missy!" Kylie screams, startling the rest of us. Then, realizing that she may have just given away her secret shame—that Zach is still a sore subject—she tries to quickly recover the situation, pretending that the Zach dig had her up in arms strictly out of concern for Zoe. "That's Zoe's brother you're talking about," Kylie says, placing her hands protectively on Zoe's shoulder.

Missy shakes her head. "Ky, you know it's true. Anyway, this girl definitely thought Zach was interested and—"

Kylie finishes the explanation. "And I saw Lexi tell her to just go for it and hook up with him! And she knew about our history. So, obviously I decided to set her friend up." Kylie shrugs. "When Denise began to suspect that there was something going on between them . . ."

Missy interjects, "Courtesy of the rumors I spread on Kylie's behalf."

"She was pissed, but she didn't actually fire the girl until well after the season ended," Kylie concludes.

"What happened then?" I ask.

"That's when I sent Denise a picture of Zachary and the girl on the beach," Kylie explains, a sheepish grin spreading across their face.

Missy pipes in. "From the angle, you couldn't tell whether they were talking or canoodling."

"And I prefer not to know which it was," Kylie says. She's so vehement that she almost makes her stool tip over.

"Don't you feel bad about getting that girl in trouble?" Zoe asks earnestly. She and Kylie are neighbors and she's always tried to see the best in Kylie despite her somewhat tumultuous past.

"Yeah, I do, actually. It was a stupid thing to do. And I regret it now. But it felt really good at the time," Kylie confesses. She looks down, clearly uncomfortable about being this honest.

"And besides, it wasn't like her summer was ruined. I hear she ended up going to France with Violet and Hannah." Missy adds. She nods, looking pleased with her ability to rationalize the situation.

"You know that's just a rumor, right?" Kylie asks quietly.

Missy shrugs, obviously unbothered by the whole thing.

"By the way, did you guys catch the way Lexi was looking at Jason?" Zoe interrupts in a desperate attempt to change the topic. She insists that she's okay talking about Zach-related drama, but I'm not convinced.

"Ha ha! I know," Missy screeches. "I couldn't tell whether she wanted to jump him or kill him." Then her eyes widen. "I wonder if she's going to ask him to the Last Blast Luau."

"She can't," Zoe says. She looks like she's about to say more when Kylie suddenly decides that it's time to leave.

"Love you and everything, Abby, but it's beach time!" Kylie calls out. She slides her oversized Dolce & Gabbana sunglasses from the crown of her head to the bridge of her nose.

"Sorry about Lexi," Missy says, even though she clearly isn't. She pushes herself off her stool as daintily as possible. "If she didn't like you before, she'll like you even less now that she's seen you hanging out with us."

"Yeah, sorry *chica*!" Kylie yells out. "Don't say we didn't warn you."

I wave goodbye to my friends and walk over to Jason, who's at the bar inputting an order. "Thanks again for your help with that table."

"No problem." Jason's hands fly across the keys.

"So, what did you think?" I ask.

"About what?" Jason finishes at the computer and shifts so that he's facing me directly.

"About my friends. They're amazing, right?"

"You think?"

"I know."

He runs his hand along the counter. "I heard you girls talking about the Last Blast Luau at the end there."

"Yeah, it seems like a pretty big deal."

Jason looks up, peeking through a tuft of dark hair. "It is. But that doesn't matter for you and me."

"What are you talking about?"

"We can't go," he says, all serious.

"What do you mean? Of course we can."

"No." Jason pauses. "We can't. The only way you and I are attending is in an apron with platters on our hands. It's a members-only event."

"What? No . . ." My voice catches in my throat. "My friends would have told me."

"They should have. But you saw how quickly they left. They knew and they decided to leave you hanging."

"No . . ." I say. My refusal doesn't sound convincing.

Jason places his hand on top of mine like a brother telling his sister that there's no tooth fairy. He looks into my eyes. "How amazing are your friends, really?"

# Chapter Ten

**"Faster!"** Denise screams. She's decided that this conditioning practice—our first—will determine who will work the beach and who
will be stuck at the pool. "Remember, ten minutes max!"

I scamper across the shore, my feet bare, refusing to let the
uneven sand slow me down. And I thought basketball suicides were
tough. After this, I'd take a pair of running shoes and the smooth
hardwood any day. My thigh muscles burn, but I'm totally in my
element. The air smells of salt and to my right waves spill across the
wet sand.

"And you call yourself lifeguards? Where did you get your certi-
fications from? The Acme?" Denise paces back and forth with an oak
clipboard tucked underneath her muscular arm.

I touch one plastic cone, turn around, and sprint to the other.
Beads of sweat build on my brow.

"I'd be nervous to set foot in the water with out-of-shape guards like you!"

This is my chance to show Denise that I deserve to be here. And it's perfect because she has Lexi off running some errand. I need to get noticed right now.

I touch the other cone and dig my toes into the sand. I push off, propelling myself forward against the wind. A few feet in front of me, a flag flaps, signaling the finish line.

"Push yourself!" Denise screams, standing with her arms crossed. "We're already more than seven minutes in!"

With the rest of the group behind me, I pump my arms and run as fast as I can. Sand sprays from my heels, pecking at my calves.

I lunge forward, first to cross the finish line. I try not to let Denise see that I can barely catch my breath. I want to her to think that conditioning is easy for me. Even if it's not.

"Impressive," Denise strolls over, eyeing me up and down as I stifle the urge to take a deep breath. There's no way I'm showing her how winded I actually am. She flips through a few pages on her clipboard. "Abby, right?"

I nod, getting my breathing under control. "Abby Berkeley."

"Abby Berkeley, eight minutes. Nice job." She pats me on the back. Then, looking at the other lifeguards struggling to finish their sprints, she says, a little loudly, "I think we can be sure that *someone* here is going to be assigned to the beach."

"Thanks." I beam, doing a little victory dance in my head. First, the beach and then the scholarship!

Denise, though, is already on to other things. She places the whistle in her mouth.

*Tweet!*

"Let's go!" she shouts. The whistle dangles around her neck. "You should all be ashamed. A new girl works harder than you!"

*Ouch.* The "nice job" would have been more than sufficient.

I bend over to touch my toes, stretching out my hamstrings. Then I grab a bottle of water from the cooler and tip it into my mouth, allowing the cool liquid to rush over me. A moment later, two guys tumble over the finish line.

*Ohmigod*, Brody. I practically spit up my water. Only . . . it's not him. It's some other guy—Greg, I think his name is. He has green eyes and a similar haircut. Weird. Where is Brody? Why isn't he out here with the rest of us? I haven't seen him at all today.

A couple more lifeguards stream past the finish line. Allison and Brooke are among them. Another guard, Tammi, follows close behind.

"Fifteen, fourteen . . ." Denise calls out, staring at her stopwatch and counting down the seconds left. She paces, scanning the few of us who've finished. "Only six out of twenty-five lifeguards have made it in under ten minutes! This is a disgrace!"

Six out of *twenty-four*. Brody isn't here.

"Come on, Zoe!" I yell. She pumps her short arms, sweat glistening on her olive skin. "You're almost there."

Zoe lowers her head like a bull, her high ponytail bouncing as she makes her way toward us.

"Five. Four. Three." Zoe crosses the line as Denise screams out the seconds remaining.

"Oh my God." Zoe falls next to me on the sand. "I think I just died a little bit."

I'm tempted to tell her, "Kind of like I did when I discovered that you, my best friend, didn't tell me that the luau was members only." But I decide now's not the time to pick a fight.

Zoe grabs a water bottle from the red plastic cooler and pours it all over her face and chest. If she notices me moving a few feet away from her in the time she does that, she doesn't say anything.

"The rest of you!" Denise yells to the group of stragglers. "Every single one of you"—she points to the exhausted guards still trudging through the suicides—"owe me extra sprints at the end of today's workout."

"Aw . . ." a few groan.

I can feel my lips start to spread into a grin. This competition is mine. All mine.

Lexi naturally chooses that time to come back from her errand— whatever it was. "What's up next?" she asks, assuming her usual position in front of Brooke and Allison.

*Oh please.*

"Did everyone hear that?" Denise shouts.

The group looks at Lexi, attempting to figure out what Denise is talking about.

"While everyone else is catching their breath and acting like a bunch of wusses, Lexi wants to know what's up next." Denise lights up, glancing proudly at her errand girl. "And that is why Lexi is the captain this year. It's all about attitude."

Zoe steps next to me. "The only reason Lexi's captain is because Brody dropped out."

"My thoughts exactly," I murmur back to Zoe, momentarily forgetting my anger. We both cross our arms and give Lexi our most piercing stares.

"You people should be ashamed of yourselves," Denise says, stomping off toward the white lifeguard tower to gather whatever equipment she needs for our next torture session.

"No. Lexi should be ashamed of herself for being such a butt kisser," Zoe whispers to me.

I can't help it. I giggle.

Lexi swings her head around like she heard us. But before she can exact vengeance, Denise returns, dragging five long ropes attached to red plastic torpedo buoys. She drops the buoys in front of us.

"Please split yourselves into groups of two," Denise says, motioning to where she wants us to stand by the buoys. "We're going to review ocean rescues today."

Zoe nudges me and I shrink back involuntarily. She still feels like a bit of a traitor. Looking around, though, I realize that the only other people I know are Lexi, Brooke, and Allison—and it's not like I'm going to partner with any of them in this lifetime—so I step forward. Might as well stick with what I know.

Zoe gives me a weird look, having noticed my hesitation, but she doesn't make a big deal of it.

I take a moment to gaze at the buoy directly in front of us. I can't help it—I'm practically bursting with excitement. I've been practicing for this day my whole life—acting out *Baywatch* episodes with Beach Barbie, dressing up as a lifeguard for Halloween, and even making my youngest brother pretend he's drowning at the community pool once so I could save him. I was asked not to do that anymore after the "real" lifeguard dove into the pool thinking my brother was in distress, but that's beside the point.

I glance from Denise to Zoe to Lexi to the club—wondering if Brody's lurking there—and finally back to Denise. Then I take a deep breath and let the moment wash over me. I slowly pick up the buoy by the side handle. I run my finger across the red plastic, imagining my first save, and in that moment I know what *the point* really is.

It's not what my dad and Jason said, not Lexi's shenanigans, not who's allowed to go to the luau, and not even what Brody's being back here means to me. None of it.

It's that I'm about to be a real lifeguard.

# Chapter Eleven

**About an hour later,** Zoe and I are practicing our saves at the end of the beach away from everyone else. Zoe floats on her back, leaning against my chest, her arms wrapped around the buoy. The tips of her pink-painted toenails peek above the water.

"This is nice," she says. "There's nothing like floating along after a tough day of training."

I scissor-kick using the current to pull us toward the shore. One or two saves is exhausting, but I lost count at ten. "Yeah, it's great. What is this, our fiftieth save of the day?"

"Lexi seems to be handling it okay," Zoe says, tilting her head to the right, where Lexi and Allison have been working on their saves a few yards away. Lexi is pulling Allison to the shore, seemingly without any effort.

Seeing how easy it is for Lexi to work in the water gives me the extra adrenaline push I need. I drag Zoe to shore in a pronounced display of fake "save-ry."

"Whoa, there," Zoe says, disentangling herself from the buoy. "What's gotten into you?"

"I can't let Lexi win."

"Ah . . . shouldn't be surprised that's your answer," Zoe says. "It's always—"

Suddenly, I can't contain it in any longer. "Why didn't you tell me about the luau?" I interject. I'd been waiting for the right moment to say something, but it's too hard to keep my frustration inside. I just have to know why my best friend let me believe a lie. "You made me think I was allowed to go."

"Oh Abs, I'm sorry. Please don't be upset at me. I've been meaning to tell you that the luau is members only, but I just knew how you'd react and . . ."

"How I'd react!?" I tread water so that we're eye-to-eye.

"Yeah, you'd think that you couldn't go."

"Obviously, that's what I'd think."

"Yeah, because your family is all a bunch of cops. You guys think that rules aren't meant to be broken."

I think back to what Jason said about the soda. "That's not true. . . ."

Zoe continues where she left off. "But they'll totally make an exception for you."

"But not for other people, right?" I feel for the sand with my feet.

"What are you talking about?"

"I'm talking about people like Jason, who only work at the bar or whatever. Are they ranked lower than me or something?"

"What? Did you swallow a sand crab this morning? You seriously need to chill out. You'll be allowed to do everything."

"One, you don't know if that's true. And two, you're missing my point. What about everyone else?"

"I dunno. Win the competition and change the rules or something."

A wave hits me dead on and saltwater runs up my nose and into my mouth.

"Abby?" Zoe asks. "You okay?"

The saltwater burns my eyes and I struggle to see clearly. "Do you think it's that simple?" I ask, rubbing my eyes.

"Maybe. Beats me."

"Huh . . ." My anger disappears as I wonder if Zoe is on to something. So, what are you doing after this?" I ask her.

"The usual—playing educational games on a four-year-old's iPad. Mrs. Johnson has a yoga class tonight. Want to join us? I could really use the extra hands."

"I . . . uh . . ." I blink my eyes a couple of times and look out by the cliffs. I think I see something dark floating there. *Is it a stingray?* "Zoe, did you see that?" I ask.

"What?" she says, turning to look the same way as me.

"Is that a body?!" she screams.

I don't stay to debate it further. My instincts take over and I swim as fast as I can, leaving Zoe in my wake.

And then I see the victim.

It's a man. Facedown. I pull his arm above his head and then turn him over just like I learned in my lifeguarding course.

Oh. My. God.

It's Brody. His eyes are closed and he somehow seems smaller than I remember him, more vulnerable. But it's definitely him.

"Ohmigod, Abby!" Zoe comes up behind me, catching sight of Brody's immobile form.

I can't find the strength to respond. And even if I did, I wouldn't know what to say.

I give in completely to my training, shoving the buoy in front of Brody and wrapping my arms around his chest. I pull him toward the shore using every ounce of energy I have left. The waves knock me off balance, but I keep our heads above the water as the current propels us forward.

Once I reach the shallow surf, my mind races, reviewing everything I learned about CPR—first assess breathing . . . *Five, breath, five* . . . I slowly drag Brody's body across the flat wet sand, laying him down as gently as I can.

Zoe reaches us at that moment. "What's going on?" she asks. Worry fills her voice.

I don't respond. I can't. The water slaps my legs as I adjust my position. I lean my ear to his mouth hoping, praying. I listen for a breath.

I get chortling laughter instead.

I jump back, startled. *"What are you doing?!"* I demand.

"Wow. Pretty impressive rescue for your first day," Brody says, opening his eyes. They crinkle as he smiles. He's been fine this whole time.

"What the hell are you doing?" I push him away. "I thought something horrible happened to you."

Brody laughs hysterically, holding his side to keep from falling over. "We'll have to talk to Denise about getting you a special award."

"All righty then. Pretty messed up if you ask me." Zoe stands up. "I'll see you later, Abs." She slowly walks away.

"Zoe, wait," I say, but Zoe's already jogging toward the tower where the other guards are drying off. I turn back to the pretend victim, my hands on my hips. "Seriously, Brody, what was that?"

"I was watching you and it looked like you needed a break," Brody says, rolling on his side. He balances his head on his bent arm and I can't help but notice how the incoming ocean water spills over his thick bicep, covering his chest and abs in a healthy sheen.

"A break?" I inch back, crossing my arms in front of my chest. "You think that me thinking you're dead is a break?"

"I dunno. I guess it was a way to snag some more time with you. You didn't seem that interested in seeing me yesterday."

I'm too angry to think about whatever it is that Brody's trying to say. "Aw . . . did that upset you? I didn't peg you for a—"

"It did as a matter of fact."

"And you thought that the way to my heart was through a panic attack?"

"It was worth a try. And honestly, it didn't really seem like you were sweating it." He reaches out to caress my arm, but I quickly scoot away.

"I wouldn't have done it if I'd thought you'd be this angry," Brody grumbles.

"How could I not be angry? Explain to me again why you thought a fake rescue was a good idea?"

"I was in the tower drawing up the schedule so that Lexi could practice and I saw you from the window. When I got done early, I thought I'd give you some real rescue experience to prep for the competition."

I feel my face heat up and it's not just because he glossed over the whole helping Lexi bit. "Yeah, that's great and everything. But it's not funny to pretend you're dying."

Brody sits up, totally serious all of sudden. "You're right," he says sincerely. "Death is never funny. Thinking about how it must have looked to you . . . I can't believe I did that. I just wanted to see you, but now that I think about it, it was stupid. I feel terrible and . . ."

"It's okay, Brody," I cut him off. "You can stop the apology."

"So you forgive me?"

"I didn't say that. I just said—"

"How about I make it up to you with dinner tomorrow night?" Brody's emerald eyes glisten.

I hear a whistle and look back in the direction of the sound. My stomach drops. Denise and the other guards are standing around. I wonder how long I have before Denise starts thinking that something's going on here.

"Brody, I really have to go," I announce.

"Okay, okay. I get it. But what about dinner?" Brody tilts his head, pulling me in with his eyes.

"It's not a good idea," I say, standing up. "What you did just now was pretty ridiculous. Plus, there's the Denise issue and you still haven't told me what's really going on."

Brody shrugs. "I think it's pretty obvious—you're here, I'm here . . ."

"Why are you here, Brody? Why aren't you at Michigan? You still haven't told me."

"I'll tell you whatever you want to know."

"You will?"

Brody nods.

"First off, why . . ."

*Tweeeeet.*

Denise's whistle cuts us off. "Bring it in!"

That does it. I give Brody a quick wave and start briskly walking back to the team. I don't get more than two steps before I hear a persistent voice call out, "So . . . dinner?"

# Chapter Twelve

**"Are you lifeguarding tomorrow?"** I ask Zoe. I'm spread across my down comforter with my phone tucked between my ear and shoulder. Even though the sun has gone down and my windows are open, I'm still sweating buckets. Mom refuses to turn on the AC unless it's above ninety, and today the temperature only reached a balmy eighty-seven. And I should know—I was outside sprinting in it.

"Yes! I just found out," Zoe screeches. "I'm working the pool in the afternoon. How about you?"

I picture Zoe resting on her enormous king-sized bed in her sub–seventy degree central air–conditioned room with views of Catalina in the distance.

"Morning at the beach," I sigh. "Suckage. I was hoping we'd be together." I feel around my neck for my friendship charm, reminding myself to leave it at home since I'll have to quickly change into my snack bar attire once I'm done at the beach.

"It's my fault. I should have tried harder to make the cut for the beach." Zoe's sigh is audible through the phone receiver.

"You'll get there. And if I didn't have to work the snack bar tomorrow afternoon, we could have totally hung out." I stretch my sun-kissed legs above the head of my bed, resting my feet against my corkboard filled with newspaper clippings and old pics.

*Bang.*

My door shakes. A picture of my brothers and me sitting on the lifeguard stand at our old beach dislodges from my collage and floats to my bed.

"What was that?" Zoe asks.

"Just Alex and Frankie wrestling in the hallway again."

I muffle the receiver and shout, "I'm on the phone!"

I'm assaulted by the sounds of laughter on the other side of my door. Then another bang.

"Sorry!" I hear my middle brother, Alex, shout between grunts.

"They're so annoying," I say. With my phone still tucked, I catch my arms on the floor and back flip off my bed. Then I stand up and fall onto my desk chair. I reach into my desk drawer to grab my planner, knowing that Zoe is sure to ask about our next babysitting engagement. My eyes land on a hotel brochure I saved from the infamous swim conference where Brody and I first met.

"So . . . did I tell you that Brody asked me out?" I ask Zoe.

"He did what?!" Zoe yells into the receiver.

"He asked me to dinner tomorrow night, but I'm not gonna go," I say even as I pull the brochure out of the drawer.

"Whatever. It's obvious he still likes you."

"I wouldn't exactly go there. Usually when normal people like each other they don't pretend that they're dead." I trace my finger along a photo of the shore where Brody and I had our first kiss.

"He was just trying to be cute! And anyway, I think it's fate. You and him ending up at the same club for the summer. It's exactly like Prince William and Princess Catherine going to St. Andrews together."

"You're seriously obsessed with royalty."

Zoe ignores me. "Brody is totally like a prince. The prince of BCC. And you're about to become the princess."

"Are you saying I come from lowly roots?"

"I'm saying that you're the best swimmer and that everyone is about to be awed and amazed by you."

"Uh. First off, let me you remind you that we just so happened to be at the same club for the summer. I wouldn't exactly call that fate. Plus, Brody and I don't even know each other. We hung out one night at a swim meet. That's it. O-V-E-R."

*Bang.*

I slam the brochure down on my desk and pull the phone away from my ear. "Stop!" I scream.

Zoe sighs. "Boy, you really have some crazy people living in your house."

"Yeah, tell me about it."

I hear my mother's stern voice behind the door.

"Have you broached the Brody subject with them?"

"It's a little premature, isn't it? Anyway, we already know what they'd say. They hate guys like Brody."

"You don't know for sure. . . ."

"Zoe, you know as well as I do that they'll take one look at Brody and see Nick. They'll think that he's super entitled and that he wants more than I'm willing to dish out."

"Brody's not like that," Zoe says. Then she screams, "Ugh!"

"What happened?" I ask, practically jumping into the phone to save my best friend.

"Just spilled my nail polish on the floor."

"Oh."

I can almost make out the sound of Zoe shrugging. "Guess it's not a big deal. I can always get the rug replaced."

"You can?" I look at my carpeting. It's dotted with the residue of hair gel left during my scrunching period, nail polish stains from sleepovers past, and even an ink stain from when Frankie decided my bedroom floor was his personal canvas.

"Anyway, back to Brody, he doesn't seem the type that'd be easily shaken. Even by your brothers." I hear Zoe pop a piece of gum into her mouth.

"Then what type is he?"

"I dunno. He just always seemed like one of the good ones." Zoe pauses. "But then again . . ."

"Yeah? What?" My heart skips a beat.

"Okay, I don't want you to freak out. . . ."

"Yeah?" I urge Zoe to continue.

"My brother told me he heard something about why Brody is back at the beach club."

"Why would I freak out about that?" I stand up and walk back to my bed.

"Well, you know, normally I'd buy Zach's stuff as just, well, Zach being Zach—super immature and egotistical and whatever. But since you're so worried about the whole playing dead thing, I figure I have to tell you. . . ."

"Tell me what?" I sit on the edge of my mattress.

"Zach said that Brody was forced to *withdraw* from Michigan—apparently because of some really bad reason." Zoe pops her gum.

"Like what?" Lots of stuff fills my head—drinking, drugs, pregnancy. Then I stop myself. This is coming from Zach.

"I don't know. I just know it's really bad," Zoe says in a dramatic voice.

"That settles it. I'm definitely not going on that date."

Naturally, my brother Frankie chooses that second to peek his head in the door.

"Hold on, Zoe." I muffle the receiver again.

"Mom has some leftovers. She wants to know if you want some." Frankie scans my room as if he's searching for something.

"Yeah. Sure," I say. "Thanks." I point to the receiver. "Phone," I mouth.

Frankie doesn't take the hint. "So, how was the old beach?" he asks, leaning against the door.

"Exactly the same except for some extra-plush lounge chairs." I roll my eyes just as my mom enters the room.

"Hey, sweetie!" my mom says, pushing the door open even wider. "We're so proud of you!"

Frankie looks down at my mom. "Uh. Maybe *you* are."

"What does that mean?" My mom stares accusingly at my youngest brother.

Frankie turns to face me directly. "Abby, you know we think you're a traitor for working at that beach club."

"Frankie!" My mom admonishes.

"What?" Frankie shrugs. "It's true. We all think that the private beach thing is completely messed up." Frankie ducks under my mom's arm and makes his way back to the chaos waiting just outside my door.

"Thanks, Mom, for being the lone person besides me in this house who thinks BCC is a good thing."

"I wouldn't go that far, honey." She squeezes my shoulder, "I'm just happy you're happy." For some reason, her words don't reassure me.

She turns to leave and I can't resist asking, "Mom, air?" I point to the unplugged air conditioner.

"It's a cool seventy-eight outside. Can't you feel the sea breeze?" She shrugs, gently shutting my door.

I talk to a closed door. "Uh, no. We live miles from the beach."

I press the phone against my ear again. "Hey, I'm back."

"It really is crazy town there. Sheesh . . ." Zoe sighs dramatically. "Anyway, since you're not going on your date tomorrow night, can you help me out with babysitting?"

I lie back against my comforter and stare at my ceiling. "Sure," I say. I've already gotten my spot on the beach so at least I can give Zoe that.

"You know, I just wanted to say how sorry I am again for not telling you about the stupid luau rules," Zoe says. She sounds as if she just sat up.

"It's okay." I play with one of the flowers stitched to my bedspread.

"No, it isn't. You're too good to me."

"Zoe, really, it's not—"

Zoe cuts me off. "The way you're so forgiving and the way you agreed to babysit just as soon as you could. That means a lot. You're really the best friend I could ever ask for."

"Ha ha . . . I doubt it."

"No, really, you are!"

But Zoe's wrong. I'm not. Because this whole time I haven't been thinking about Zoe. Or babysitting. All I've been thinking about is that photo of the ocean and how I'd give anything to be back there with Brody.

# Chapter Thirteen

**Early the next morning,** I block my eyes from the hazy sun and stare up at the massive wooden lifeguard's chair. In that moment, everything that's bothering me—the club rules, the chaos in my house, my babysitting appointment with Zoe, yesterday's encounter with Brody—all seem to disappear.

This is it. Everything I've worked for since I took my first swimming lesson at age three. I'm a lifeguard.

Above me sits an older bronzed girl with polarized sunglasses. Her platinum blonde hair is pulled tight in a short ponytail and a whistle rests between her pink lips.

One thing they didn't teach us in lifeguard training was how to climb to the top of this white stand. Good thing my brothers and I used to scale fences when we played jailbreak back in elementary school. I take a deep breath and hoist myself up. Here goes nothing.

When I reach the seat, the girl glances at me.

I cringe, wondering if she's anything like Lexi. From the looks of the schedule, the two of us are going to be together for most of the summer. And if she's as ridiculous as my sorry-excuse-for-a-captain, I'm in for a long two and a half months.

The girl—Katie according to the sign-up list—kindly smiles at me. Then her eyes trail off and she resumes scanning the surf. "Are you Abby?" she asks, adjusting her wrap-around sunglasses.

"Yup. And you must be Katie," I say, attempting to shove my bag underneath the chair like the other lifeguards. But, try as I might, it doesn't fit. I think about all the things I threw in there before I left the house—my snack bar uniform, an apron, a pair of sneakers. Things the other lifeguards don't have to deal with.

I resign myself to plopping the bag behind me. Then I adjust my bathing suit, and settle in next to my partner.

"Nice to meet you," Katie says. The sun reflects off the silver whistle dangling around her neck.

*Oops.* My whistle. How could I forget my whistle? I turn around and unzip the front pocket of my bag, shoving my hand inside.

"What are you looking for?' Katie asks.

"My . . . uh . . ." I thumb through the front pocket, feeling around my swim goggles. I don't want to tell my partner that I forgot my whistle on the first day. She'd probably report me to Denise immediately.

"Abby, you okay?"

I unzip the middle section and dig through my apron and clothes. If Zoe and I were on the same shift, none of this would matter. I wouldn't have to impress anyone. I could just laugh it off as a silly little mistake. *But noooo . . .*

"Abby?"

I find it. Finally.

I take a deep breath and sit up, placing the whistle around my neck just like Katie.

"A little nervous?" she asks.

A cool breeze blows off the ocean. "Is it that obvious?" I ask, shivering. I awkwardly look around for a better spot to put my bag, wondering if they factor the lifeguarding equivalent of bedside manner into who wins the scholarship. So far, I certainly haven't won at any points in that area.

"You can hang your bag on the back of the chair if you can't fit it underneath the seat." Katie points to the spot.

"Thanks," I say, taking Katie's direction. I steady myself on the high chair. The waves crash and spray below us.

"Is this your first time guarding?" Katie asks. She grabs a bottle of SPF 30 and slathers herself as she talks, never taking her eyes off the beach.

"Yeah." My eyes fix on a little girl in a butterfly bathing suit. Her swimming tube bounces as she runs toward a wave then retreats.

"You really are nervous, aren't you?" Katie asks.

"Do you think that little girl is okay?" At training they told us that a tube usually indicates the little ones can't swim.

"She's fine," Katie reassures me. "It's the kids who don't show fear that you really have to worry about."

"Oh . . ." I say, confused. Part of me wonders if maybe Katie is just taking the easy way out. "So, um, have you been doing this for a while?"

"You could say that."

The girl sits on the sand, stretching out her tiny legs in the shallow water. I relax. A little.

"I remember my first day on the job," Katie begins. "I noticed a boy—he must have been five-years-old—drop his swim trunks and start peeing in the ocean. So I jumped off my chair and ran toward him as fast as I could."

"His mom must have liked that."

"Ha! I wish. She got mad at me when her kid burst into tears after I directed him to the bathroom."

"Really?"

"Yeah, she was all, *How dare you mess up my son's self-esteem?*"

"Because it takes a lot of courage to pee in the ocean . . ."

Katie laughs at that one. "Exactly! Definitely big-man-on-campus material. Anyway, suffice it to say that my first day was not pretty. I almost lost my job over that one."

"Wow," I say. "Tough break."

"Tell me about it." Katie smiles. "And I'm still here."

*You wouldn't be if you weren't a member*, I almost say.

The warm sun moves behind a cloud, sending a chill into the air. Goose bumps appear on my legs. "So, if I manage to successfully stay away from peeing boys and girls in swim tubes, what *do* I have to be worried about?"

"Basically, our job as lifeguards is to prevent something bad from happening." Katie pulls out a red lifeguard hoodie from her bag. "Rip currents are the biggest threat for a drowning. That and alcohol. People always act dumb when they've had too much to drink."

Katie stands up and blows her whistle. She waves her arm, signaling a couple to move away from the rocks.

The guy and girl look up. They begin to move closer to shore.

Katie sits down again, satisfied that the pair is no longer in harm's way. "Look at that guy! Yeah, man!" she exclaims, pointing to a surfer skimming the top of a decent-sized wave. She practically bounces in her seat as the wave crashes over him.

"Do you surf?" I ask, looking at Katie with new eyes.

"Yup. I spend most of my time when I'm not guarding at Surfrider. The waves there are amazing."

"I used to surf here as a kid," I volunteer.

"Really?"

"Yeah." I stare at the fog on the horizon. "This used to be my family's favorite beach."

"Cool." Katie scrunches her lotion-covered nose as she gazes out at the water.

"So, you said you've been doing this for a while. How long is that?" I ask. Another gust of wind whips by, pulling a few flyaway hairs from my pony.

"Three years. I just graduated from Upper Crest."

*Upper Crest!* I resist the temptation to pepper her with a million questions about Brody. Instead, I begin with a more neutral topic. "Oh, do you know Amber McDonald?" I ask. "I played softball with her at Beachwood."

"Yeah. Love Amber. I had Mr. McDonald, Amber's dad, for history. And of course, Amber was a phenomenal pitcher. I heard she did an amazing job for you guys too this year."

"Yup. We won the invitational and saved our softball program because of Amber." I see a guy with messy brown hair tossing a football and my thoughts immediately turn back to Brody.

I know I shouldn't say anything to Katie, but . . . *she has to know him.* They just graduated together. They've been lifeguards together for years. She'll know if he's a player. She might even know what's up with Michigan.

I decide to take a super stealthy approach. "So, did you compete in last year's Last Blast Competition?" I ask.

"Came in fourth," She pauses, waving at the little girl in the butterfly bathing suit. "I just found out that I'll be leading a team this year."

Okay. That didn't exactly elicit any Brody-related conversation. *Hmm . . .*

I press on. "That's awesome. And did you attend the Luau after the competition?"

"Yeah, uh, it was fun," Katie replies, obviously distracted. "Look at this little guy." Katie points to a little boy with only one water wing. "He's the one to watch. He just tossed off one of his floats and now he's attempting to pull off the other."

A Spider-Man arm swimmy floats over a wave.

"He wouldn't have them if he didn't need them."

Sure enough, as soon as the words are out of Katie's mouth, the boy's mother joins him in the water, shoving the swimmy back on his arm.

"So I know someone else from Upper Crest," I finally say. I watch the little girl with the butterfly bathing suit jump into an oncoming wave. She reminds me of myself a few years ago. Except, I would have been out here with my three older brothers tossing me around.

"Who?" Katie asks.

"Actually, he works here too. But I didn't know that until the other day."

"Oh, really? Then I'm sure I know him. What's his name?"

"Brody Wilson?" I say, more like a question than a statement.

Katie's face lights up. "Of course I know Brody. Everyone knows Brody. He's—" Katie interrupts herself, catching sight of two boys chest-deep, throwing around a football by the cliffs. She stands up and blows her whistle, putting more oomph into it then I realized she had.

"There's a definite pull toward those rocks today. Must be some sort of weak current." Her voice takes on a more serious cast. "You always want to make sure no one gets anywhere near the rocks or the cliff. See that red flag out there?"

I nod.

"No one should get near that flag, but most bozos do." Katie sits back down. "It's especially important that no one go past it if there's a rip current. That's just dangerous." She shakes her head, then resumes the small talk. "So, if you know Brody, you must also know Lexi Smalls?" She eyes me strangely.

I gasp, almost choking on the air caught in my throat. "Why do you say that?"

"Oh, you know . . ." Katie begins, her tone implying more than she's letting on. She settles on an explanation. "They run in the same circles, Lexi and Brody. You've heard they used to be together, right?"

I cough. "Uh, no? I didn't." I cough some more.

"You okay?" Katie asks, handing me a Nalgene bottle from her bag. "Want some water to clear your throat?"

"No, no. It's okay. Just swallowed weird."

Katie hands me the bottle despite my resistance. "Anyway, I

guess it makes sense that you wouldn't have known about their relationship. They broke up freshman year."

"Who ended it?" I practically whisper.

"Brody. Lexi tries to play it off, but I don't think she ever got over it."

"You don't?" The sun reappears and I can feel beads of sweat begin to dot my back. I take a sip of water.

"Lexi is used to getting whatever she wants and Brody was the first thing in her life she couldn't get." Katie takes her hoodie off, placing it behind her. "Anyway, who can blame her? There aren't many girls here who haven't fallen for Brody."

"Really?" I say, between coughs. "So, he's a player?"

"No. I wouldn't call him *that*."

*Then what would you call him?*

I decide to just be direct. "So, why isn't Brody at Michigan?" I ask, catching my breath. I wipe my sweaty palms on my shorts.

"Oh. Yeah. That," Katie mutters, watching the water. "Word is whatever it is, his family does not want it getting out."

Zach must be right. It has to be bad. Really bad. I wonder if it has something to do with Lexi. Maybe he even came back for her. . . .

I take another sip from the Nalgene bottle.

Katie glances at me. "Look. I don't know what your deal is with Brody, but it's obviously something since you're asking so many questions about him."

"Oh, no, I . . ."

Katie cuts me off. "He's awesome and all, but I heard that you're already on Lexi's radar because you beat her at an invitational last month."

"I . . . uh . . ."

Katie waves her hand, silencing me. "It doesn't really matter to me, but if I were you, I'd just stay away from Brody. At least until the summer is over. Lexi will make your summer here a nightmare. Plus, if Denise catches you two together, you'll lose your job."

I gulp, forcing the water stuck in my throat down my esophagus.

# Chapter Fourteen

**Nine hours later,** I've never been so exhausted in my life.

As if working a four-hour lifeguard shift with Katie wasn't enough, I then spent four hours at the snack bar listening to Jason's usual tales of beach-club bigotry and now I'm bussing tables at the Dolphin Restaurant. And not by choice. The regular day-shift bus boy was fired two hours ago after a customer complained. Yup. One complaint. Gone.

I'm about to dump the last two glasses into the plastic tub currently balanced on my hip when the restaurant manager walks up to me.

"I need you to clean up by the pool before closing time," he says, pointing at the disheveled pool area.

*Clean up by the pool? I thought I was done after the night-shift bus boy shows up.*

"Sure," I say, mustering up the best smile I can when all I really want to do is go home and sleep. Between this grueling day and Brody never showing up to explain himself, I'm wiped. And I haven't even had time to think more about the scholarship.

I walk into the hectic kitchen and dump the glasses into the sink. Then, with the tub still stuck to my side, I trudge through the side door and back outside.

After the picturesque California summer day, the pool area is destroyed. I tuck my messy hair behind my ears and focus on tackling the clutter. I pick up dirty plates, cups, spoons, knives, forks, and glasses and drop them into the container. If I keep this pace up, I should be home in no time.

That is until I run right into Brody.

"Whoa. Easy superstar," Brody says. He's wearing a lifeguard hoodie that hugs his bronzed neck.

"Hey," I say, reaching for a dish left next to the still churning Jacuzzi. My stomach swirls like water bursting from the jets. "Sorry. I didn't see you there."

He grins, showing off his perfect white teeth. "Ready for tonight?"

"I told you I'm not going." I shove a wine glass into the tub, careful not to break it. I resist the urge to ask him where he was all day.

"Fine. So I'll meet you at . . ."

"Obviously, you're not used to being told no," I say. "I'm not going."

Brody grabs my arm to stop me from cleaning. "You owe me a chance to explain."

"Uh. I don't owe you anything." I whisper just in case anyone is within earshot.

"Abs . . ."

"I'm insanely busy. The regular bus boy at the Dolphin was fired and I'm stuck cleaning the pool. Plus, I really haven't had any time to shower or change," I say, motioning to my chocolate-stained apron. "I don't think—"

"You look amazing." Brody places his hands on my shoulders. I practically jump from the electric shock.

Denise's face seeps into my mind, followed by the faces of my three brothers, Jason's, and finally Lexi's. I step backward. Brody's hands fall off my shoulders. "I can't."

He's not discouraged. "Well, then I guess I'll have to help you out so you can finish faster. Four hands are better than two," he says, waving one of his hands as he picks up a plate with the other.

"Really, that's nice of you and everything, but . . ." My voice trails off when I spot the restaurant manager talking with the hostess. I grab the plate and glass from Brody. "But it's my job and I'll get it done."

"Okay, but then I don't want to hear any excuses about not having enough time to meet me." Brody crosses his arms and narrows his eyes, pretending to give me a really stern look. It only lasts for a second before his true eagerness shines through. "How about when you're done, you meet me at the tennis courts? That way, you don't have to worry about changing for dinner."

"It's more than that, Brody." I scurry away from him, grabbing a glass off a table.

Brody picks up a lounge chair, swings it around, and straddles it. "Then tell me what it is."

I glance over my shoulder to where the hostess and manager

were standing. The manager is gone. I place the tub on a table. "Even if I did go with you tonight, don't you think the club is a little too public?" I whisper.

Brody's eyes widen. "One night alone with me last month and now you want some more private time. . . . Abs, I thought you were a good girl."

"Oh my God, I didn't mean it that way." Immediately, my cheeks heat up.

He stands and places the chair back. "The tennis courts it is. Meet me in an hour." He points his index finger at me, playfully pushing my nose. "Now make sure you show up. Don't go skipping out on me."

"Wait . . ." I whisper. But Brody scampers toward the beach before I manage to come up with another excuse.

I pick up a dirty fork and toss it in the tub, getting some leftover ketchup on my finger. Gross.

I rub the ketchup on my apron, adding red smudges to the existing palette of chocolate, mustard, and grease. It takes a second for the ketchup to come off my hand completely and I nearly stamp my foot—I can't believe that this is what my life has come to.

I look toward the shoreline and see a girl in a two-piece Speedo sprinting. A guy lounges on the sand with a stopwatch, timing her. They're too far away to make out their faces but they look they're having a ball.

*Why should everyone else get to have all the fun?*

Oh well, I guess I can give Brody a few minutes to explain why he's here and not at Michigan. He may turn out to be a huge jerk, but anything's better than cleaning up other people's leftovers.

\* \* \*

**When I'm finally finished** cleaning up the pool area, I dash into the locker room, ignoring the poster for the Last Blast Luau that someone has plastered on the door. Plush white and navy couches are scattered across the sitting area. Beyond the couches, a crystal chandelier hangs in the center of two rows of chrome sinks.

I drop my bag next to a sink and splash cool water on my face. Leftover sunscreen beads up on my cheeks as I wipe my face clean with a white towel that I grabbed from one of several wicker baskets. I gather my hair on top of my head and secure it with a black hair band. Then I step in front of a full-length mirror located at the edge of the room.

It looks like I've been sprayed with red sauce and splattered with grease. I use the towel to clean myself up. Then I let out a breath.

Here goes nothing.

As I'm walking toward the side door that opens up to the tennis courts, I convince myself that this is not a date. Brody just wants to fill me in on whatever deep dark secret lurks behind his emerald eyes.

The door shuts behind me and I'm surprised to discover that the entire outdoor tennis area—eight courts in total—is totally deserted. At first, I'm impressed with Brody for picking such a perfect hiding spot. High fences surround the illuminated courts and thick palm trees provide additional security. But my awe quickly turns to frustration. Brody is nowhere to be seen.

Nice. First, he picked college girls over me, then he claimed that he got me a job, then he acted all secretive for God-knows-what reason, and now I allowed him to stand me up. What was I thinking?

As I'm about to begin my walk of shame back to the locker room, I notice a manila envelope hanging from the intercepting chains of one of the fences. *Abs* is scrawled across the front.

I tear open the envelope and peek inside to find a navy blue bandana. I pull it out and discover that a note, *Wear Me*, is attached.

Huh, Brody didn't ditch me. . . . But if he seriously thinks I'm covering my eyes with some bandana, he's been out in the sun for way too long. Bandanas are on my father's long list of unsuspected weapons. Apparently, they've been used to strangle and gag people. No way am I setting myself up to get raped, killed, or stabbed.

I ball up the bandana and stuff it back in the envelope when I hear a familiar husky voice call out, "I was worried you wouldn't come."

I scan the courts. Still no sign of Brody, but his voice sounds close by.

"Uh, I'm not gonna wear a blindfold. The only way I'm putting on this bandana is if I'm using it as a headband." I search for Brody through the palm trees. The leaves sway in the gentle ocean breeze. "Why don't you come out of your little hiding place? This is freaking me out."

"I promise it'll be worth it," he says.

I look around again, trying to determine the direction his voice came from. The beach, maybe? I walk up to the gate and crack it open, surveying the surroundings. The wooden walkway to the beach is completely empty.

"You think?" I ask, waiting to follow the sound of his voice.

"You'll see . . ." His voice fades away before I can make out where it came from. "Just think of it as a game. You're an athlete, you must love games. . . ."

"I love games? I think it's the other way around." A shiver runs up my spine.

"Shh . . . You're gonna be sad if you ruin the surprise. Just tie the blindfold around and let me do the rest."

"How about I just cover one eye?" I mockingly cover my eye like I'm about to read an exam chart.

"Just trust me," he whispers.

"That's not exactly the best line to use on me right now, Brody."

"If you see me, will you do it?"

"Maybe." Tingles of anticipation shoot through my body. I spin around, making a last-ditch attempt at figuring out Brody's hiding spot.

And then, suddenly, Brody is standing behind me on the walkway. Instinctively, I set up in the self-defense stance I learned at the police martial arts course my dad drags me to.

"Well, here I am." He steps toward me. He's wearing long khaki shorts and a black Dri-FIT Nike tee that hints ever so slightly at the muscular contours beneath.

I ease out of my stance and let out a sigh. "Okay. A deal's a deal." I shrug, never one to chicken out. "Here goes nothing." I wrap the blindfold over my eyes, leaving the bottom open a bit so I can still peek out if necessary.

Brody steps behind me and takes the edges of the bandana from my hands. "I knew you could do it," he says, tying the blindfold gently.

The feeling of his hot breath against my neck sends me into a nervous titter. "My basketball coach made us do a teambuilding activity that started out like this too," I blather.

"Well, here's hoping that this is a bit more fun." He places his strong hands on my hips and begins to guide me forward.

"Where are we going?"

"You'll see," he says, whispering into my ear. Tingles erupt from the top of my head to the tips of my toes.

"What about your explanation?"

"We'll get to all that," he whispers again. "As soon as we get to our destination."

I step off the wooden walkway and feel the soft and lumpy sand underneath the soles of my Nikes. With each step, the swooshing waves grow louder and louder.

Brody continues to move me at the hips. "Step up," he instructs.

I step on what feel like worn wooden steps.

"That's it. Two more," Brody says, still guiding me.

"Where are we?" I smell salty air and can hear water slapping up against something.

Brody lets go of my hips. "Don't move." His cologne tickles my nose.

I feel his hands behind my head, untying my blindfold. The bandana falls, grazing the back of my shirt as it floats to the ground.

When I open my eyes, I'm standing on a wooden pier. The smacking sound I heard is the waves lapping against a dock. A small white motorboat with a pale blue canopy idles in front of me. I look up at the ebony sky peppered with white twinkling stars.

"Ready for our night together?" Brody asks, holding out his hand.

"Wait." I look down at my stained shorts. "I don't know if I'm really dressed for all this and what about Lex—" My earlier attempts to convince myself that this isn't a date seem more like self-delusion than ever.

"You look perfect," Brody says.

"Liar," I say, more like a joke than an accusation. I breathe in his scent—it's musky, manly, delicious—and suddenly I'm back at the swim meet. In that second, all of my anxiety—about what everyone would say, what Lexi would do, how Denise would react—all of that just disappears. Somehow nothing—not my annoying brothers, not babysitting, not even Brody's strange reappearance and his earlier refusal to commit—seems to matter anymore.

All that matters is this one moment.

I clasp my hand around Brody's and he pulls me on the boat.

# Chapter Fifteen

**Brody cuts the engine** about half a mile from the pier. The entire time we've been on the water, we haven't said two words. And now I'm offshore in the dark with Brody, a boat, and his big secret.

He walks to the back of the boat and tosses the anchor.

"I didn't know you had a boat license," I say as he passes me.

"There's a lot you don't know about me." Brody sits on a white leather seat next to a large straw picnic basket that he brought along with us. He leans back, his long arms sprawling across the padded bench. The glow from the boat's deck light shines on.

*He's got that right.* I turn around from my seat at the front of the boat. I want to see everything—every grimace, every adjustment, every clue—before I ask the big question. "So . . . why are you here?"

"What do you mean? Hanging out with you?" He grins mischievously. "You shouldn't have to ask."

My cheeks redden. "No, not that. Why aren't you at Michigan?"

"About that," he says, suddenly serious.

I nod. "Yeah." I lean forward waiting for his confession. Ten bucks he says, *I came back because of Lexi.*

He pauses. "It's really not a big deal. I'm staying local. Taking some classes at the community college this fall. I'm in the process of applying to UCLA for the spring and so, uh . . ." He opens up the top of the picnic basket and rummages through it. "Just forget about what I said that night. At the meet, I mean."

*Wait. What?* "Uh . . . That's it?" That doesn't sound like anything super scandalous. Maybe he's just afraid to tell me the real reason. I decide to lay my cards on the table. "What about Lexi?"

"Lexi? What about her?" He looks up at me. His emerald eyes turn forest green in the dark.

"Didn't you guys . . ." *Wait. I'm not pathetic.* "Never mind." I'm totally confused at this point. I thought he was *forced* to withdraw. Or at least that he came home because of some secret romantic tryst.

"So tell me about swimming. How's it going?" He hands me a plastic container.

I decide to let my suspicions go for the time being. "Great. Actually that's the easy part of lifeguarding, the swimming and conditioning. It's more the working two jobs and feeling like a total—" I stop myself. What am I doing opening up to him again? "What's this?" I ask, staring at the container he just handed me.

"Last time I checked, it's food," he says, smiling.

I place the container on my lap and pop it open. "How did you know I love chicken Caesar salad?"

"And raspberry iced tea." He hands me a Snapple bottle.

I eye him sheepishly.

"Remember, you told me?" Brody says, popping open his own container.

"Look, Brody, I really appreciate the dinner and everything. . . ."

He continues to rummage through the picnic basket, pulling out napkins and another Snapple for himself.

"But do you really think this is a good idea? I mean, what about the club's rules?" Silently, I think, *And what about what my family would do if they knew I was on this boat right now?*

Brody shoves the basket on the boat floor, leaving an empty spot next to him on the leather seat. "What about them?"

I don't know whether the gesture was meant as an invitation, but I ignore it regardless. "I really need my job. And I'm not sure that . . ."

He holds up his sandwich in a sort of "cheers" motion and starts to chomp down steadily.

I forget what I was about to say and we're silent for a few seconds.

"Anyway," I say, staring at my salad. My stomach rumbles. I'm absolutely famished after working for so many hours and the dressing smells good.

"It's not poisoned," he says between bites.

"Isn't that what they all say?"

"They?" Brody shrugs.

"The bad guys who lure helpless girls out to their boats and—"

"Abby, let me stop you right there. I don't know if you've noticed this about yourself, but you're not exactly what I'd call 'helpless.'"

I grin despite myself. I like that Brody's noticed that I'm no damsel in distress.

"Look, I've been meaning to talk to you about that night at the swim meet," he says, washing down his sandwich with a swig of iced tea.

I stab my salad with my fork.

"When I met you that night, you were . . ." He pauses. "Different."

*Different? Is that supposed to be a good thing? Different from who? Lexi?*

"You actually listened to what I had to say. We like the same things. It was insane meeting you like that." He swallows. "Except the timing was horrible and then I couldn't shake you. Everywhere I went all I saw was you."

*Wait. That's exactly how I felt.*

"And then everything changed, and I . . ."

Hold on. I need to focus. My brothers warned me about guys like this. Guys who are too smooth to be real. This is the kind of thing Nick used to do—shower me with sweet talk just to try to get something from me. I used to fall for his lines all the time. But now, I—

"I really think you have a huge chance of winning that scholarship and I'd love to—"

*Scholarship? Huh?*

Brody is interrupted by a boat tearing across the water. It rocks our small motorboat, causing me to dump the contents of my salad onto the deck.

"Oh my God, I'm so sorry. . . ." I try to shovel the salad back into the container with my fork.

"Don't worry about it." Brody kneels down and begins wiping the floor with napkins. "It's no big deal. I'll just spray the deck down when we get back."

But it *is* a big deal. What if Lexi was on that boat that just went by? Or worse, Denise? What if someone else sees us out here and reports us back to them?

"Brody, we have to head back," I say, completely serious.

"Wait. What?" Brody stops wiping and looks up at me. "It's just some lettuce. No reason to—"

"Brody, I want to go."

A hush falls over our boat. "Are you sure?" he asks, slowly pulling up the anchor. His disappointment reads clear on his face.

"Positive."

The boat's engine roars to life and we head back to shore as quickly as we came.

**We reach the dock** and Brody wraps the rope around the pylon.

"Thanks for dinner. I'll see you later," I say in a rush. I climb out from between the seats and am about to step off the boat and onto the pier when Brody grabs my arm.

He looks deep into my eyes. "Abby, I'm not sure what happened out there, but I don't want to leave it like this."

"There's nothing to 'leave.' We had a nice night last month and I got caught up in the moment just now. But that's it," I stammer. "I really gotta go . . . ." I step out onto the pier.

Brody follows after me. "Look," he says, his hand dropping from my arm. "Forget about us for a second. You need to go after that scholarship. You have a huge shot of winning."

"Uh . . . okay." I feel my cheeks heat up. This is the second time Brody's mentioned the competition. "Thanks for the advice. I'm flattered. Really. But—"

"Let me train you."

"What?" I nearly stumble into the gap between the boat and the pier.

"I won last year. I know how this place works. Let me help you."

"You want to train me? Seriously?" I cross my arms.

"Yeah, I do. I want you to be happy, to go after what's yours. And if you let me train you, that scholarship is yours for the taking."

The thought is tantalizing, but I force logic to win out. "No, it's not. Not if people start to think that there's something between us. I'll get kicked off the team."

"Abs, there *is* something between us." He does that thing again where he widens his eyes and peers into my soul.

"See what I mean? There you go again, with your lines and your—"

"It's not a line. But how about if I promise that absolutely nothing will happen. I'll keep everything strictly professional." He takes two steps away from me.

As if the distance will keep things totally PG. Please.

"I appreciate the offer and everything, but I gotta go."

"Abs, wait!" Brody shouts.

I'm already off and running toward the tennis courts. As exhausted as I am after working for hours today, every fiber of my being knows that I have to get away from Brody to clear my head. When I reach the courts, I lean against the fence and slide to a sit. I breathe a sigh of relief. I'm finally in the clear.

But then I catch a whiff of familiar cologne. I hear a hushed voice. It's earnest but firm. "I thought you'd do anything to win."

And with that, I know that my decision has already been made for me.

# Chapter Sixteen

*Eighteen.*

I tuck my body into an underwater somersault. Then I roll and push off the concrete wall. As the water rushes around me, I turn and begin my dolphin kick.

*Only two more.*

Denise called a mandatory conditioning practice after a rumor took flight that two unnamed lifeguards were spotted hanging out late last night. The guys are in the gym and the girls are in the club's indoor lap pool. I, meanwhile, am in total misery—there's still no word on whether the rumor in question actually involves me.

"Let's go!" Denise yells. Her voice echoes across the vast pool room. "It's the first week and I've already had to field questions about our guards! Already!"

I kick harder, gliding through the water, but my freestyle is sloppier than normal. All I can think about is how angry people are going to be when they find out it was me who caused the extra practice, let alone that I accepted Brody's offer to train me. I'm so consumed by these thoughts, in fact, that for the first time in a long time, I suck in water instead of air. The chlorine overpowers me and I flail around, gasping for breath. It takes a few seconds to regain my composure and I begin my stroke again.

I glance over at Lexi as I'm about to flip into another turn. She somersaults seconds before me.

*Oh no you don't.*

I tuck and turn for the nineteenth time and push hard off the side, streaming through the water. I pull my arms, gliding as far as I can. Underwater I see Lexi's toned frame inches ahead of me.

I come up for air, stretch, and begin my freestyle. The rhythm of my stroke pulls me into my zone.

I kick harder and faster. *No need to fight the water*, I hear my rec coach's words echo in my head. *Relax and move with the flow.*

"Tight finish here for first!" Denise's voice booms through the pool house.

Lexi and I are matched stroke for stroke. I shut my eyes, concentrate, and dig deep. Then, right before I stretch my body and pull my lead arm toward the finish line, Lexi splashes water into my face.

I breathe it in by accident and begin to choke.

*Ahek . . . Hack . . .*

"Lexi by a touch!" Denise says, clapping her hands. "Way to go, ladies." She's totally oblivious to Lexi's tricks.

My chest burns as I slide my goggles on top of my swim cap.

Lexi hangs on the side of the pool, her arms outstretched like she owns the place. When Denise walks away, she glares at me.

"Hate to break it to you, *ma barista*, but you'll never beat me in the water." She doesn't show the least bit of shame about splashing water in my face.

I wipe my face and breathe deep, clearing my nose and throat. "The only way you'll beat me is by cheating like you just did. But believe me it won't happen again," I say, hoisting myself out of the pool. "Consider that a gift."

My feet leave wet footprints as I walk toward the pool locker room. While I wait for the others to finish, I tear off my goggles and launch them against a locker. I grab my phone from my bag and begin to text Brody. I mean, if Lexi is just going to cheat, then I might as well get a jump-start on our training sessions.

I stop myself as I'm about to hit send. Who am I kidding? *I can't train with Brody.* I'm probably already about to be reprimanded, and what if Denise finds out that I'm meeting Brody for some one-on-one sessions? I wrap a soft towel around my waist, sit on a bench, and bury my head in my hands.

My thoughts begin to race: What if Denise saw me and Brody together after all? What if she was the one on the boat?

I should have just ignored Brody. One night with him and I'm already dogging it at practice. I lost to Lexi. And I never lose. Why did I ever agree to go on that boat? Why didn't I listen to Katie? This is just ridiculous—I've worked my whole life to be a lifeguard and suddenly a boy comes along and I agree to do things *his* way. After Nick, I should know better.

I wipe my face with the towel and let out a deep breath. Then I snatch up my bag and walk back to the pool.

Out of nowhere, Zoe appears in front of me. "Where were you last night?"

"What are you talking about?" My stomach drops to the damp floor. "Did Denise—"

"Babysitting! You told me you would help me out." She violently grabs a towel off the shelf and wraps it around her waist.

Oh God. I hadn't thought about that since I arrived at my first lifeguarding shift.

"I'm so sorry, Zo. I totally forgot. Brody showed up to help me while I was cleaning up the pool area and asked me to go on this boat with him and I . . ."

"Brody?" She re-ties her towel, more gently this time. "You could have texted, you know." My answer seems to have satisfied her.

"I know. I really just forgot. I've been such a—"

Zoe holds her hand over her mouth. "*Ohmigod.* Do you think this punishment conditioning is because of you and Brody?" Her earlier sternness is replaced with deep concern.

My stomach lurches. "Maybe . . ."

"Well, you better hope it's not." Zoe nibbles on her nail. A pool of water begins to form underneath her. "Denise will fire you."

"Thanks for pointing out the obvious." I inhale deeply as if I'm about to hold my breath underwater. I let it out in a rush. "I just don't get it. Why is she so hung up on this stupid rule?"

"I don't know, but are you ready to face the music?"

"I guess." I shrug.

Zoe and I step out of the locker room to discover that the pool area is completely deserted. We scurry toward the other side of the room, passing some posters for the Last Blast Competition and Luau along the way.

Maybe the other guards are already in the gym?

But no. As soon as we make our way into the hallway, we're met with screams. They seem to be coming from Denise's office. We back away.

Through the glass window, we can make out Brooke and Denise sitting on either side of Denise's desk. Anyone else would be cowering, but Brooke sits tall, calm. She seems to be taking Denise's reprobation in stride.

"You think you're going to show up to a conditioning practice you caused and just phone it in?"

"I didn't," Brooke counters, still cool as a cucumber.

"You didn't what? Come in last place at the practice just now because you weren't even trying? Or hang out on the beach after hours with another lifeguard?"

"How do you know I wasn't trying?"

"How do I know you weren't trying . . ." Denise mutters under her breath, facing the back wall. She turns abruptly back to Brooke, slamming her fist against the desk. Zoe and I jump. "I think you're missing the point, Miss Lauder. I specifically laid out the rules and you decided to disregard them the first week you're here. What do you have to say for yourself?" Denise's hands are on her hips.

Brooke doesn't even attempt to save herself from Denise's fury. "Maybe you're the one who needs to be hanging out with someone from the wrong side of the lap pool." She winks.

Denise goes completely red. "Turn in your uniform to me

tomorrow morning. You're done!" She turns and storms out of her office.

It doesn't seem like she plans to take Brooke's advice.

Slowly, some of the other lifeguards start to come out of their hiding spots. Zoe and I weren't the only ones eavesdropping, apparently. I nod at Katie who seems baffled for the first time since I met her. Lexi and Allison ignore me.

Brooke emerges from the office.

"What the heck did you do?" Lexi asks.

"Nothing. I just hung out with Greg on the beach for a bit. We talked. It was harmless."

I wonder if Brooke and Greg were the couple I saw timing each other.

"Yeah right," Lexi says, rolling her eyes.

"Lexi!" Katie shouts. "She said she wasn't doing anything."

"Butt out of it, Katie. I think I know Brooke a little better than you." If Lexi were a cartoon character, she'd be flaring her nostrils.

Allison gathers strength from Katie's chastisement. "Lexi, seriously? You're the last one who should be saying anything." She wraps her arm around Brooke defensively.

Brooke shakes her off. It's clear that she doesn't want anyone's pity. She turns to Lexi. "At least Greg is a . . ."

Lexi shoots her a look that could smother fifty-foot waves.

"Never mind," Brooke mutters. She pulls her towel tighter around her body and storms back into the pool area, presumably to head to the locker room one last time. The rest of us are left staring at Lexi.

I salivate with curiosity, desperate for someone to finish where Brooke left off. *At least Greg is a what? A friend? A boyfriend? A nice guy? And what does that make the other person she was referring to? A Brody?*

Assuming that I'm not about to be booted from the team, I really can't handle any more bombshells about Brody. . . . You know, now that I've agreed to train with him.

"Whatever." Lexi rolls her eyes at the ceiling. "She's always been such a drama queen." She hightails it toward the gym.

*Talk about the pot calling the kettle . . .*

Allison's eyes shift, flipping back and forth between the pool area—where Brooke is packing in the attached locker room—and the gym—where we're supposed to begin the next stage of conditioning. Finally, she trails behind Lexi. But her usual gusto isn't there.

"What was that all about?" I ask Katie.

"Is Lexi hooking up with another lifeguard?" Zoe's eyes widen.

*Please don't be Brody. Please don't be Brody.* It has to be Brody.

"I don't know." Katie shrugs.

"It sounds scandalous," Zoe whispers, secretly loving the drama.

"In the gym. Now!" Denise's voice booms through the hallway.

Katie, Zoe, and I sprint to the door, the two of them visibly shaking as if they're the ones in trouble.

But they don't know what trouble is. They're not the new girl—the non-member—who's about to begin secretly training with one Brody Wilson.

# Chapter Seventeen

*Clang.*

My mother's long blonde hair tickles my shoulder as she sets a dish down in front of me. The aroma of fresh-from-the-oven turkey breast and double-baked potato rises from the steamy plate.

I've spent the last few weeks guarding the beach with Katie, listening to Jason's grumblings as I fill orders at the snack bar, and training with Brody nearly every night after work. At this point, I'm famished.

"Dinner looks awesome," I say, reaching for the gravy bowl. I smile widely, hoping that a cheery exterior can mask my big deceit.

I'm still torn about whether I should tell my parents about training with Brody. He was right. It *has* really been helpful. And, at my insistence, totally platonic.

But I don't think my family would understand why I need the additional insider assistance. It'd be impossible for them to accept that my technique—unlike Lexi's and some other guards from the club—is at a disadvantage because I haven't trained with Olympic medalists. They'd probably just laugh at me and tell me to practice some more at our local rec center.

But I can't just do some laps and be all set. I'm desperate for the scholarship and someone needs to show that Lexi girl what's up. I don't care that she probably only won during that conditioning session because she cheated; I can't risk it happening again.

"Thanks," my mom says, setting another dish at the head of the table in front of my father. "You let me know when you're ready and I'll show you how to make the turkey."

"As soon as Frankie joins me for the cooking lesson," I say, pointing at my younger brother's empty seat. "Where is Frankie?"

"Frankie! Dinnertime!" my dad bellows down our short hallway.

As I pour the brown gravy over my turkey, my mom takes her seat across from my father and between Alex and me.

"So, Alex, I heard wonderful news. Is it true that the police department might be hiring next year?" My mom beams as she reaches for the gravy. "That would be just in time for graduation."

My middle brother, Alex, looks up from shoveling potatoes into his mouth. After his recent buzz cut, his blue eyes are particularly prominent, matching his police academy cadet uniform. "We'll see. Not getting my hopes up especially with all the recent layoffs."

My dad shakes out a cloth napkin and shoves it into the top of his starched white shirt. "Times are tough, son."

"And that's exactly why I'm starting my landscaping business after graduation. No way am I risking my life on the streets just to have the state lay me off." My youngest brother pulls out the chair next to me. His wild curly hair is extra poofy today.

"Nice of you to finally join us, Frankie," my dad says curtly.

Ever since Frankie grew out his hair and announced his plans to cut lawns for a living instead of joining the academy, my dad hasn't exactly been pleased with his youngest son.

The static of the scanner cuts in. *Four. Seven. Eight. Six.*

"Where's Robby?" I ask, attempting to pull the conversation away from my favorite—equally "rebellious"—sibling.

Just then Robby rushes in.

*Three. Fifty-one. Alpha.*

Robby's leather belt squeaks as he leans over and kisses my mother. "Sorry, Ma. I got a call." He removes his police hat before he sits down.

My dad stops as he's about to shovel turkey into his mouth, eyeing me as if for the first time. "You've been home late for the last few nights. I feel like I haven't seen my little girl in ages. What's my fish been up to?"

"Yeah, Nemo." Frankie chuckles next to me. "What have you been up to?"

I smack him in the side. "Nice fro, clown," I say, pointing to his dirty blond ringlets. "I'm good, Dad. Just working hard, that's all. Putting in extra time so I can win the scholarship I told you about."

"Did you put in a twelve-hour shift yesterday? I don't even make my guys work that hard and they're grown men." My dad wipes his mouth with the napkin.

I concentrate on cutting my turkey. "Just a long day. That's all."

"What, are they running some sort of sweat shop?" My dad snorts. "I still don't understand why you want to be a part of all that."

"Let us know if they're overworking you, Abs," Robby chimes in. "Don't let those people push you around. And if you don't feel comfortable sticking up for yourself, let us know. We'll take care of them."

"Yeah. Not gonna happen to a Berkeley." Alex stabs his baked potato with a knife.

I keep my eyes on my plate and wait for the onslaught to pass. Eventually, my brothers will begin arguing with each other. And then, I'll be left to ruminate over whether there's any chance of making this training thing work for much longer without crashing and burning like Brooke. That, and how nice it's been to see Brody's green eyes every day.

"Do any of the other lifeguards have to pick up second jobs?" Alex asks.

I shake my head no, bracing myself for their reaction.

My mom comes to my rescue. "I think it's great that Abby's working so hard at what she's passionate about," she says, smiling supportively at me. She breaks her roll in half.

"Thanks, Mom," I say, glancing up for a moment.

"There's a perfectly good swim club right down the street," my dad contradicts. He turns to my mom. "And anyway, our daughter isn't exactly passionate about bringing hotshots their curly fries."

"Yeah, but I'm working the beach. Our old beach. What could be better than that?" I ask.

"Working somewhere where people value you for your skills

and not your ability to wait on them hand and foot." My dad bangs his glass against the table.

"Mom, can you pass me the gravy again?" I ask, desperate for them to talk about something—anything—else.

My mom's lips move into a relaxed grin. "Of course." She hands me the bowl.

"Can they really do that, Dad?" Alex looks at my dad with total reverence, eager to hang on every word.

"I think it's something that we definitely need to look into," my dad nods. He turns to me. "Abby, forget going with Zoe tomorrow. I'm going to drop you off before my shift and talk to the manager."

"What?!" I screech. "No. You can't do that." I eye my mom, silently pleading for her to save me.

She shrugs. She doesn't like to get in the way of my dad when he gets this overzealous.

My dad lays his palm over the top of my hand. "It's for your own protection, Abigail."

I pull my hand back. "Before you guys get your pants in a knot about my new job, I wasn't exactly working the whole time yesterday. Or the day before . . ."

"What?" My father stops chewing and wipes his mouth.

"I was with someone." My nerves cause the words to tumble out of my mouth before I can stop them.

"You were with someone?" Robby repeats.

"Who?" My father asks, leaning forward on his chair. His large frame casts a shadow over the table.

I calmly pour gravy over my potatoes wondering what I should say next now that I opened my mouth. I settle with, "Just someone."

"A boy?" my mother asks.

I don't answer, but my brothers take my silence for a big *yes.*

Alex piles on first. "Do you even know this guy, Abby?" he asks.

"How could you be so stupid?" Robby admonishes. "I just picked up a homicide victim the other night for hanging out with 'just someone.'"

"Is he some rich jerk?" Frankie demands.

"Frankie, watch your mouth at the dinner table." My mother lets out a sigh. "And will you guys give Abigail a chance to explain herself?" She looks at me. "Now tell us about this boy, honey."

The scanner on top of the refrigerator cuts in, giving me time to think. *Last Name. Gerger. George. Edward. Roger. George. Edward. Roger. One. Eight. Six. Zero. Three. Two thousand. Nine. Lexus.*

I don't manage to come up with anything. "His name is Brody." I swirl my gravy with my fork.

"Brody?" Alex drops his knife. "That's a sissy name."

I squeeze my fork.

My dad leans briskly back on his chair and rubs his hands over his face as if trying to wake from a dream—or really, a nightmare.

"Sounds like that douche from that show *The Hills,*" Frankie adds.

"Is he like that, Abby? I swear if he touches you . . ." Robby says.

I ignore them. "He's the guy I met at a swim meet last month. He's sweet. He's actually been . . ."

"And he's a member of that ridiculous club you're working for?" my father asks, knowing full well the answer.

"Yeah." I shrug.

My dad grabs his napkin from his collar and throws it onto the table. "Here we go. This is exactly why we should have never agreed to send you to Beachwood Academy. I should have listened to my gut and not let your mother talk me into it."

Robby pulls out the small notebook he uses for work and flips it open. "How do you spell his last name?"

"You are not doing a background check on my boyfriend. . . ." I stutter. "I . . . I . . . I mean, a guy I know."

"Boyfriend? Brody's your boyfriend!" My mom places her hands in front of her mouth. "You must invite him over."

Fat chance.

"Wait a second. At the invitational?" My dad asks, mumbling to himself something about a hotel and minors.

My mom ignores him. "At least now I know why you were moping all over the house after the meet."

Robby continues his interrogation. "So this guy. He makes you feel bad about yourself, huh?" He eyes me suspiciously from across the table.

"What, are you practicing so you can make detective in a year? Knock it off."

Frankie chuckles next to me.

"And no, he doesn't make me feel bad about myself. It's the opposite."

By this time, my father's fists are clenched. My mother glances nervously from me to him.

This is not good.

My mom makes a last-ditch attempt to save me from the squabbling. "Your father was saying that there's a scholarship this club is offering. What's that all about?"

"It's an amazing opportunity. I've—"

"You're not going to win." Robby cuts me off.

I drop my fork and wrap my arms tightly across my chest. "Oh yeah? Shows what you know." I turn to my mom. "Actually, Brody has been a big help."

"I'm sure Brody is just dying to help you with all kinds of things," Alex smirks. "I swear, Abby, if that guy tries anything on you, like that Nick piece of . . ."

"Oh, for Christ's sake. I think I've heard enough." My father holds up his hand in the stop position. "Abby, as your father and as a police officer, I think I know a little something about men. And I'd bet you anything that this Brody boy is going to try to take advantage of you just like everyone else at that club."

"That club? That club?" I stand up and violently push in my chair. "You don't know anything about that club. All of my friends are members of *that* club. You guys need to seriously lay off."

"Sweetie," my mom says. "Don't leave. You didn't finish dinner."

Robby lets out a loud breath. "Friends, huh?"

"And what do you mean by that?" I glare at Robby.

"It means that you're fifteen years old and you don't understand the meaning of the word *friends*," he says smugly.

"Shut up, Robby." And without thinking about how this might not help my maturity cause, I pick up my spoon and launch it at him.

Then I storm out of the kitchen and slam my bedroom door behind me.

# Chapter Eighteen

**"Five more!"** Brody shouts.

My thighs burn worse than my sunburned shoulders as I squat and squeeze a medicine ball during another training session at Brody's beachfront backyard. The waves crash against the sand a few yards from us. To our other side, Brody's lap pool gleams in the Malibu Colony sun.

"Two. One," Brody counts down.

I let out my breath, bend over, and roll the heavy rubber ball toward him. He tosses me my towel.

"Tired yet?" he asks, before beginning his own sets.

"Nope." I wipe my face and think about how we've been able to pull this off. Somehow, Brody and I have settled into a routine—a routine that consists of lifeguarding at the beach, working at Sunset, and then slipping into Brody's Jeep unseen for a two-hour training session at his house.

I almost spilled the beans to my parents last night, but still, by some great stroke of fortune, we've managed to conceal our plans from prying eyes.

I don't let my blowup with my parents get to me. I pick up a plastic jump rope off the concrete and begin cardio.

*Tick. Tick. Tick.*

I stare at the white stucco exterior of Brody's three-story beach house. This place is truly paradise. At least from the outside. I haven't exactly made it inside yet.

"Fifteen," Brody says, after he finishes his reps a minute later.

"Ready for your swim?" Brody asks as he sheds his tank top. I sneak a peek at his chiseled chest and rock-hard abdominal muscles.

"Always," I say, dropping the rope.

As Brody lowers himself into the pool, I climb out of my Nike shorts and tank, and adjust my purple two-piece. I toss them on a lounge chair, along with my running shoes and socks, and grab my swim cap and goggles.

Once I'm in the water, I tuck my hair underneath my cap. Brody skids a kickboard across the water toward me.

"A kickboard?" I ask, ready for my regular routine of freestyle laps.

"It works to strengthen your kicks," Brody says, lying across another board.

"I know that. But didn't I work out my legs enough today?" I play around, balancing on the board with one hand.

"This is better."

"You think so? Why don't I just swim laps?"

"Trust me." He wades over.

I lean over the board and smile coyly at Brody. "I'm getting there." Which is true. During the past few weeks, Brody has done just what he said he would—trained me. No games. No moves. No playing. Well, maybe a little flirting.

But nothing serious. I saw how badly my family reacted when I just hinted at the possibility of something going on between me and Brody. Besides which, I don't want to give Denise any extra ammunition.

Or Lexi for that matter. I still can't shake the suspicion that something is going on between the two of them.

Brody adjusts my position, even though he really doesn't need to, moving my hips with his hands until I'm balanced on top of the board. "Kick as hard as you can for an entire lap. Lean across the board and don't use your arms at all. Rely only on your legs. Kicking is your power."

"My coach always told me my stroke was my power," I say, purposely being difficult.

"You'll see." Brody playfully splashes water on my face.

I feel foolish on the blue board, but I begin to kick, recognizing that even though it's fun to give Brody some push back, he really is my best hope of winning the competition. Already, he's shaved a few seconds off my one hundred meter freestyle time.

The water sprays around me like a fountain. Since I've already been working my legs for an hour, it feels like a weight's attached to my ankles.

But I won't dare admit it.

When I reach the end of the lane, I let go of the board. It pops out of the water and lands on the cement next to Brody, who's squatting at the side of the pool watching me intently.

Brody looks up from his crouch. "Is that all you've got?"

I splash water on him. "You've been saying the same thing for the past week and a half!" I mock him with a squeaky voice. "Is that all you've got, Abs? Is that all you've got?"

He holds up his hands to block the spray. "Well, I'm waiting."

"Waiting for what?" I ask.

"I'm waiting for you to take it to the next level."

"You'll see me take it to the next level, don't you worry. Just you wait till the competition. I'll take it to a level your girl Lexi has never even dreamed of."

Brody lowers himself into the water. "Lexi isn't my girl."

I duck underneath the water until I'm parallel to Brody.

"You are," Brody says once I reemerge.

A chill runs down my legs. It's all I can do not to swim into his arms at that very second. I shake myself. "Enough of this talk. Race me!" I taunt, gently pulling Brody's dark goggles over his eyes.

Brody's eyes flash with glee at my touch. "How about if I win, you'll go to the Last Blast Luau with me," he says.

"But . . ." I'm about to say that I don't even think I'm allowed to go, but I stop myself. If I win the competition, they'll have to let me go to the dance. But what will they say if I show up with Brody? I hesitate, shaking my legs underwater and adjusting my swim cap.

"Deal?" he says, moving toward the block.

"Fine." I roll my eyes.

"Ready. Set . . ." He sets himself up to push off. "Go," he shouts.

I push off the side with all my strength, submerging myself in the water. I reach out, straighten my body, and glide. My arms form a triangle as the bubbles from my nose and mouth tickle my face.

My legs slice the water like scissors, propelling me forward as my arms find a perfect rhythm. As always, I shut my eyes and sink into my zone. This race is mine. I'll show Brody.

Sure enough, I reach the other side first. I grab the edge of the pool and pop my head out of the water as Brody's hand comes into view.

I pull my goggles over my swim cap.

"That was easy," I say, pumping my fist. "Abby, one. Brody, none. No Luau."

"Not quite. I saw you tap. I was definitely done first." Brody smugly smiles.

"No way!" I catch my breath. "Anyway, you were fighting the water. I had better form, stroke, kicks. It was all me," I say, slithering away from the side. I grasp the blue-and-white plastic rope that divides the two lanes and resist the urge to pull him closer to me. Only a mere few inches divide us.

It seems that Brody can sense my longing because a second later, he wraps his arms around my waist, pulling me toward him.

Off in the distance, a siren screams.

I jump, pushing Brody off me in a panic.

"What was that?" Brody asks, dumbstruck as I dart to the side of the pool.

"Uh . . . nothing." I peek between palm trees, expecting to see Robby or my dad barrel through the back door ready to arrest Brody. They'd probably bring along a bogus charge, like Abby endangerment.

"Doesn't look like nothing, Abs. What are you on the Most Wanted list?"

"You could say that," I say, holding on to the rope.

The siren fades. In its place, the sound of waves crashing and a pelican squawking seem to become more acute.

I pull myself out of the water. I start to make my way over to my stuff when the French doors to Brody's patio open. A woman with a high blonde pony dressed in gray shorts and a T-shirt walks out onto the terrace. In one hand, she carries a Windex bottle.

I let out a breath, wishing that I'd met Brody's mom under other—less wet—circumstances. "Hi, I'm Abby. It's so nice to finally meet you." I hold out my hand.

"Oh. Hi, Abby. It's a pleasure to finally meet you too," Brody's mom says. She gently smiles. "I've heard so much about you."

"Brody, do you want anything to eat before I run errands for an hour or two?" she asks.

I'm surprised by how young Brody's mom looks. But then again, Zoe's mom had a bunch of surgeries two years ago and looks a lot younger than she used to too.

Brody looks at me. "Do you want anything to eat?"

I shrug, wrapping the nearest towel tightly around me.

"No. We're good. Thanks," he says, dunking his head in the water.

"I'll see you later then."

"Where's mom?" Brody asks.

Wait. Mom? I thought she was his mom.

"Your mom is in the master suite resting," the woman retreats back into the house.

I glance at Brody. "That wasn't your mom?"

Brody chuckles. "My mom? Julia is like thirty-two. No. That was my housekeeper."

"Oh," I feel my cheeks flush. "So where's your mom?"

"Julia just said. Sleeping."

"I'd love to meet her someday," I announce. I surprise myself with my brashness. This is the first time I've mentioned his parents. I'm all too aware that discussing his family life could lead to revealing information about my own. And that could definitely be a recipe for disaster, considering their collective hatred for all things Malibu Colony.

Brody shrugs and looks away. "She's really busy most of the time."

"How about your dad?"

"They've been divorced since I was little." He looks up at the sky. "So, when am I going to be invited to your house?"

"I doubt you would want to meet my family," I say. "They're a little different."

"Different how? Are *they* the ones on the Most Wanted list?"

"Heh . . ." I giggle nervously. Stalling for time, I wring out my hair.

"Jeez, Abby. Maybe you should go . . . I'm not sure I should really be associating with the daughter of criminal masterminds," Brody jokes.

"No, no, it's the opposite." *Did I just accidentally convince Brody Wilson that my family is a bunch of crooks?* "My dad and brothers are police officers." I cringe, waiting for his reaction.

Brody hangs on the side of the pool. "Your dad and all three brothers?"

"No, just the one so far, but the middle one is in the academy. My youngest brother wants to do something else."

"That's cool."

"That's cool?" I say. "You're not freaked out?"

"Why? Should I be?" He smirks.

"I guess not," I say, picking at the Mickey Mouse ears on my Disneyland towel. Unlike at the club, here I bring my own. "It's just that my dad and brothers are a little overprotective."

"An overprotective family isn't exactly something to be ashamed of."

"Yeah, but most guys are a little weird about the cop thing."

"I'm not most guys."

He can say that again. I toss my towel to the side and dive into the pool, eager to finish my laps now that we've gotten all of that Dr. Phil stuff out of the way. When I emerge from the water, Brody is inches from me. His green eyes glimmer.

He pulls me toward him. "And since we're asking questions . . . How come after spending nearly twenty-five hours training together just the two of us, you still won't let me kiss you again?" His breath is hot against my neck.

"I'm not most girls." I giggle, mocking him. Goose bumps dot my legs.

"I know." Brody whispers in my ear. "That's why I like you so much." He lingers for a moment gently, his lips millimeters from my skin.

Oh. My. God. As I'm about to give in, I pull away.

I turn around, hoist myself out of the water, and sit on the edge of the pool. Still immersed in the water, Brody rests his arms and chin on my lap.

Suddenly, I'm overcome with a sense of perspective. "Thank you," I say, removing his arms from my lap.

"For what?" He watches me lower myself into the pool again, my skin prickling like it's being tickled with a feather.

"For training me and pushing me and calling me out when I'm dogging it," I say. "This competition means a lot to me. I really want to win that scholarship."

"It's been my pleasure."

I quickly kiss him on his damp cheek. "There's your kiss."

"That's not the kiss I'm talking about," he says, taking me into his thick cut arms.

I wiggle away from his grasp.

"You know, you're my favorite client," he says, smirking at me as I stand up.

"I'm your only client," I say, rolling my eyes. "So is this really what you're going to do with your life—become a personal trainer and try to hook up with all your trainees?"

"I would probably make a lot of money."

"Please . . ."

"You know I'm good."

"Race again?" I say, stretching.

"So I can *let* you win a second time?"

"Oh please." I playfully punch him in the shoulder.

Brody unexpectedly takes a turn for the earnest. "What do you say you go to the Luau with me for real? The competition will be over. You'll be declared the winner. And the rule won't matter anymore. You can change things."

I drop my head. Brody only said exactly what I'd been hoping for, but still, I feel the fun and lightness of the evening being swept away like a dark storm cloud. "Brody . . ." I pause. "I told you. I can't." I stare at the calm pool water.

Brody lets out a deep breath. "Really, Denise won't care anymore."

"It's more complicated than that . . ."

"What are you talking about? What's complicated about it?"

"For one, what if I'm not asked back here next year? They'll never rehire me if they know about us."

"Many other places hire lifeguards."

"Not with my friends and my beach." I wade through the water away from him. "I'm sorry," I say, my shoulders sinking.

"Don't say you're sorry," he says, coming up behind me.

"But I am." I turn around.

He lifts up my chin with his finger. "I should be the one saying I'm sorry. I know how much this scholarship means to you. But, after you win, all bets are off and I'll get you to change your mind."

"Doubt it," I say. But what I mean is *Yes, you probably will.*

# Chapter Nineteen

**"I still can't believe** we're going to the Santa Monica Pier tonight. What are we, tourists now?" Missy complains as my teammates from school and I stroll across the wooden overpass that connects the wide pier to Ocean Avenue.

"Oh, come on. It's a tradition! We always hit the pier to watch the fireworks," Kylie reminds Missy.

Aromas of seafood, pizza, cotton candy, and Mexican food mingle with the salty sea scent as we near the pier. I nibble on my nails, too preoccupied with what happened at yesterday's training session with Brody to truly appreciate a fun Friday night with my B-Dub teammates. Up ahead, Pacific Park's roller coaster rattles across the tracks. Their world-famous Ferris wheel's flashing lights brighten the dark sky.

"I can't remember the last time I was here," Missy says as the strong sea breeze tosses her wavy blonde locks. "I think I was six."

"Um, Missy, it was last year," Taylor timidly corrects her.

"Lame," Missy says, while checking out her French manicure. "Tell me again why we're not shopping at the Promenade?"

"Oh, stop complaining, Miss. It'll give you wrinkles," Kylie answers, sagely.

"You know you secretly love roller coasters," Amber volunteers from her spot up at the front of the pack.

"Yeah, as much as you secretly love the bartender from the beach club," Zoe adds, giggling.

I notice that she's wearing a new necklace instead of her matching friendship one—she must have bought it with her babysitting money. Come to think of it, mine is still sitting in my drawer.

"You got that right. That boy is hot with a capital *H*!" Missy laughs.

"Just remember, he's mine!" Kylie says, hip-checking Missy into a group of incoming joggers and roller bladers.

Everyone laughs at this, but I'm having a hard time getting into the excitement. I feel like there's a giant current pulling me away from these girls. But mostly it's my fault. I still haven't told them about my training sessions with Brody. I want to, really, but they all have such big mouths—Kylie especially—and I can't risk confiding in them.

Their convo continues without my input.

Missy fires back. "I don't know Miss Collins. You seem to be claiming a lot of boys lately. I saw you getting down and dirty with one just last night."

"Oh. My. God." Amber turns around from the front of the pack. "Who with?"

Kylie ignores her. "First off, there's no getting down and dirty with me. I've got class." She mischievously grins. "But don't worry, that doesn't mean I can't have a little fun. . . ."

"Hey, look, you can see the fireworks from here!" Zoe exclaims. As much as Zoe tries to play it cool with Kylie, I know she still feels a little weird about her dating other people besides her brother. Even if she *is* the first to recognize that Zach is a total jerk.

"I love fireworks!" Amber echoes Zoe's enthusiasm.

Missy rolls her turquoise eyes.

I can't muster the appropriate level of elation, so I decide to quietly ask our six-foot basketball starter about her boyfriend. "Where's Matt?"

"Working," Taylor says, gathering up her brown hair in a high ponytail. "He got a summer job working at the medical rehab center his dad is staying at. He wants to be able to keep him company."

"Aw . . . Matt's such a good guy," I say.

Taylor's cheeks turn the color of cotton candy.

Just then, Brooke jogs by us, her long brown ponytail trailing behind her.

"Hey, Brooke!" Kylie shouts.

Brooke, dressed in Nike shorts and a pink sports bra, turns around and jogs in place. She pulls a white bud out of her ear.

We all crowd around her.

"Have you heard from Denise?" Zoe asks.

"Is she going to let you back on the team?" I add, thinking about my own indiscretions.

Brooke stops for a second and stretches her quads. "Are you kidding? And even if she offered, I wouldn't want back on. Getting kicked off that squad was the best thing that happened to me this summer."

*Wait. What?*

"I'm so over all the stupid rules. I don't know what I was thinking before, limiting myself because of some job." Brooke stretches her neck. Then she crosses one arm over the other to get a deep stretch. "Now Greg and I do a whole lot more than just *talk*, let me tell you." She winks at us and jogs away.

We stand in silence for a moment.

"What was that?" Zoe finally says.

"She has a point," Kylie adds, twirling a piece of blonde hair around her index finger. "I don't know how you guys deal with Denise."

I deal with Denise because lifeguarding is my dream job. I would put up with a shark if I had to.

"Ready for Pacific Park?" Amber walks backward in front of us. Her auburn pony and hair ribbons blow in her face.

I glance at Zoe. "Race you to the roller coaster."

"Wait!" Kylie screeches. "We can't hit the rides until we eat. I've been dying for a meal since softball practice," Kylie says, stopping in front of the Mariasol Restaurant at the end of the pier. "How about some Mexican?"

"Mexican food before the rides? No way. I'll puke my guts up," Zoe says.

"Come on," Kylie whines.

Missy grabs my arm. "Not before we know the latest." Then she turns around and stares at me with her cool blue eyes.

I feel my face heat up. "Err . . . What?"

"Abby has become super secretive when it comes to Brody lately," Zoe exclaims.

"That's probably because of that ridiculous rule Brooke was just complaining about," Kylie adds, tucking a piece of blonde hair behind her ear. "Who does Denise think she is, telling the lifeguards what they can and can't do after hours?"

Missy eyes the rest of us knowingly. "Kylie has been giving a lot of thought to after-hours activities lately."

"Huh?" says Amber in confusion.

"Because of her own," Missy clarifies.

Kylie saunters along coyly as if there's no way we'll be able to get the deets out of her. Clearly, this must have something to do with what she was hinting at a few minutes ago.

"What have you been doing?" Taylor asks, the bewilderment clear in her voice.

"More like who." Missy giggles.

"Brett Davidson." Kylie stops mid-stride, raising her eyebrows in triumph.

"You and Brett Davidson?" Amber's eyes are the size of the softballs she hurls faster than a car speeding down the freeway at four in the morning.

"I don't know how everyone missed Kylie's slick moves in the lobby at the club last night. She sucked Brett's face off in front of everyone," Missy says.

"You what?" I ask, hoping to keep the attention on Kylie.

"What Missy said," Kylie says, her eyes glimmering as she scans the group. She catches sight of Zoe's wide-eyed expression and, mistaking horror for encouragement, she wraps her arm around my best friend. "Question, Zo?"

Zoe struggles for something to say. "Uh . . . how was it?"

"Oh, it was goooood. Hot and heavy and delicious." She lets go of Zoe. "I'll leave the rest to your imagination. Now, let's grab some grub."

"What?!" we all screech.

"My Brett-kissed lips are sealed," Kylie smirks.

"I'm starving for an enchilada," Taylor says, heading toward the door.

Amber holds the door for us as we enter Mariasol. I file behind Missy and Kylie, thrilled that I somehow managed to get off so easily. As I'm squeezing inside, a little boy walks into my leg, throwing me back a step. When I regain my balance, Missy stops in front of me suddenly.

"Is there any room up there, Miss? I can't move in here," I ask, getting a whiff of Missy's Dior perfume.

"Oh no she didn't," Kylie growls under her breath.

*Didn't what?*

Missy turns around to face me. She's quickly followed by the rest of my friends.

"What do you guys think about Bubba Gump instead?" Missy asks, grabbing my arm. She pulls me toward the door I just fought to enter. "I just love their shrimp."

"What's going on?" I ask amid the confusion. Customers dart at me from every direction.

"Sounds like a great idea." Zoe nods. She points to the door. "I wasn't really in the mood for Mexican."

"Perfect," Missy says, pulling me again. She motions for the other girls to follow us.

But when Amber moves to the left to join us by the door, I see what they're all shielding me from.

From across the restaurant, Brody and I spot each other at the exact same second. His face drains of color. "Abs," he mouths, looking like he's spotted a ghost.

Next to him is a luscious blonde in a cheerleader hoodie. Her arm comfortably snakes around Brody's bicep.

Zoe grabs my other arm to steady me. Kylie, meanwhile, puts her arm out in front of me to keep me from lunging at him through the crowd.

"Are you guys in line?" a man shouts behind us.

A baby cries.

My eyes move from Brody to the girl then back to Brody again.

I bolt down the pier.

# Chapter Twenty

**"Abs, hold up!"** Brody's voice echoes behind me.

My flip-flops clunk against the uneven planks. The awkward movement causes my feet to slide and graze the rough-hewn wood. For the first time in the last couple weeks, my knee twists and throbs.

"Abby, wait!" Brody calls out, louder this time.

I run as fast as I can. Two women pushing strollers look up at me like I'm about to snatch their babies. Behind them, an artist painting a small portrait holds tight to his canvas as I fly past.

When my feet can't take the pounding anymore, I duck behind a sign for a souvenir shop. I bend my leg, pulling on my foot and stretching out my quad.

Seconds later, Brody runs by me. He stops a few feet ahead of where I'm hiding. He squints and surveys his surroundings as his chest vigorously inflates and deflates.

I turn my head away from him, hoping he won't spot me.

"Abby, I can see you, you know," his voice rings out.

I sheepishly step out into the open.

"I take it you never won hide and seek," he says serenely. "What do you think, if you don't see me, I can't see you?"

"It was worth a try." I shrug.

"What's up with the sprint?" he asks. "Training without me now?"

I can't help it. Cynicism creeps into my voice. "Don't you have a cheerleader you have to hang out with?"

Brody looks genuinely confused. "What are you talking about?"

"That girl I saw you with. I don't want to keep you from her. You're obviously a very busy boy. And to think that you almost had me convinced . . ." My voice trails off.

"Had you convinced of what?" Brody raises his left eyebrow.

"Ugh!" I stamp off, my heart banging inside my chest. I barely get two steps before I turn back around in disgust. "Let me guess, did you offer to train her too? Is that your line, playa?"

My phone buzzes. I glance down at a text from Zoe. She tells me that she and my friends have gone to Bubba Gump after all and that I should meet them there when I'm done giving Brody a piece of my mind. She also asks if I'm okay. I quickly reply.

"You mean my sister?" Brody replies, rubbing his chin.

"Really, Brody? The sister excuse? I might be younger than you, but I'm not stupid." I lean to the side and examine the girl Brody was waiting in line with. She's chatting with a group of girls outside Mariasol. Naturally, Lexi is among them. I ignore her—I've had enough of Lexi to last a lifetime—and concentrate on the girl. She looks nothing like Brody. "I'm sorry. I've been to your house countless times and I've never seen a sister hanging around."

Brody crosses his arms across his chest. "Then go ahead. Ask her." He steps to the side, clearing my way to the girl.

"I don't need to ask her. I know enough."

"Do you?" Brody's eyes narrow, and for the first time since I've known him, he actually looks disappointed with me.

Before I can say anything, though, a fat seagull swoops down. I duck out of the way as Brody reaches over to cover my head. I catch another whiff of his Drakkar cologne. He doesn't usually wear it during practice.

I can feel the heat slowly begin to sear through my chest and I take a few steps backward, away from Brody's protective form. "I better get back to my friends," I say. I'm tempted to tell him to forget about our training sessions as well, but my heart won't let my mouth utter the words. I have to win that scholarship if I'm ever going to have a shot at a four-year school.

"Look. We're both here. And my sister—she really is my sister by the way—can hang out with her friends for a while," he says, placing his hands on my shoulders. "I think we need to talk."

"Let's say I believe you. And I'm not saying that I do." I take a few more steps back to make my point. "But it's too public here. Remember what happened with Brooke and Greg?"

Brody clears his throat, looking over his shoulder at Pacific Park. "Well, what about the Ferris wheel then? It'll just be the two of us."

"I really should go," I say, taking a deep breath. If the girl was Brody's sister, wouldn't Amber have known? Presumably, they all went to Upper Crest together, didn't they?

"No one will see us up there," he continues to plead. "You don't have to worry about being spotted and we can finally get a chance to talk . . . in private."

I look back at the girl; her straight blonde hair looks nothing like Brody's tousled brunette tresses. "We talk plenty at training. And I think we should leave it at that."

"That's not really talking though, is it?" He looks so sincere it's hard to believe he's lying to me. But my brothers—and Nick—have taught me better.

"Brody, I'm sorry, but I just don't think it's a good idea."

"How could one ride on the Ferris wheel be bad?" The light from the fireworks illuminates his green eyes. "You and me being high up in the air, gazing at the scenery?" He pauses and adopts a softer tone. "You? Me?"

I melt, ignoring the part of my brain that insists—courtesy of Jason—that people like Brody think they deserve to get whatever they want. "Okay. One ride," I give in. But, I'm pretty sure I'll come to regret my decision.

**"Orange or yellow?"** Brody asks as we wait our turn to board the Ferris wheel.

"Huh?" I'm looking around frantically, concerned that one of Denise's moles has already spotted us.

"Orange or yellow?" he asks again. "What color car do you think we'll get?"

"What?" I stammer. I shouldn't be here. I should have gone with my gut.

"If you guess the right color, then you're a free woman. If you guess wrong, then you'll have to come to the Luau with me."

157

"Brody, don't start that again." I shake my head. "You still haven't told me about your 'sister.'" *Or much of anything else*, I think. But I don't want to press my luck family-wise. Right now I have the upper hand, but the last thing I want is for my family's disapproval of all the things he stands for to come out.

"Deal?"

"Uh . . ." I look up at the cars circling around. The Ferris wheel creaks as it makes its way to a stop, the cars above us swaying back and forth like a bunch of individual pendulums. "Yellow," I finally say, my urge to compete overriding my willpower. As soon as the word is out of my mouth, I turn around and place my hands over my eyes. "I can't look."

*Clang.* The Ferris wheel squeaks to a halt in front of us.

"Orange," Brody shouts. He holds his hands up in victory. "Looks like you'll be going to the Luau with me."

"I didn't actually agree to that, you know." I saunter past Brody and the attendant, ignoring their respective attempts to assist me, and slide into the car.

Brody settles in next to me, looking a little embarrassed that he didn't have a chance to play the chivalric knight, and the Ferris wheel begins to rotate. I scooch to the other side of the plastic seat and look out at the crowds to my right, giving Brody the silent treatment.

He quickly fills the conversational void. "It was a tacit agreement. You entered into a contract with me by voting on the color of the car."

I turn to face Brody directly. "Whoa there, Mr. Wilson. Slow down with the lawyer talk."

Brody's cheeks redden. "Sorry about that. Bad habit."

"Yeah, I bet." I pause, apprising Brody. "I thought you wanted to be a personal trainer? I had no idea you were thinking about law school."

"I'm not. I wasn't kidding about wanting to work with athletes."

"Yeah, we all know that's why you *really* wanted to train me." I jokingly punch Brody in the shoulder, surprising myself with how quickly I've managed to get over the possibly fake sister routine.

"Nah, it's just an added bonus."

"So if you don't want to be a lawyer, then how do you know all that stuff?"

"You could pick up that jargon from watching television . . ." His voice trails off.

"But you didn't, I'm guessing?"

The Ferris wheel jolts to a stop to let another couple on board. Our car rocks back and forth, and I can feel the wind on my face. I shiver and pull my jacket sleeves over my hands.

Brody looks out at the people below us. They've already begun to seem like miniature toys. "No, I didn't."

"So, then, how?"

"I've just been around a lot of lawyers." The Ferris wheel cranks as it starts up again.

My stomach drops as we resume our ascension to the top. "Because of your parents' divorce?"

"Yeah . . ." Brody turns back around to face me directly. "So I guess now is as good a time as any to tell you about Mara."

"Mara?"

"My sister—the girl you saw before."

I mentally revisit my initial impression—the girl's coloring looked nothing like Brody's, but were there other features I ignored?

"Yeah. She lives with my dad in Brentwood when she's not at boarding school. Has ever since my parents split up." He pauses. "The divorce left us all pretty torn up—lots of lawyers, lots of baloney—so we never really used to talk much. She basically has no relationship with my mom."

"Oh." I stare at Brody, really stare, taking apart the features that have become so familiar to me—his firm chin, his defined cheek bones, the way his brows are set—yeah, I can see the resemblance there.

"We've had a lot going on with my family—or what's left of it." Brody looks down at his hands. "So, um, Mara and I thought it was as good a time as any to catch up." He stops talking.

I wait for him to elaborate—to tell me whether his family problems have anything to do with why he's not in Michigan—but there's total silence on his end. Clearly, that particular conversation is over.

Fireworks sparkle across the sky, sending streams of red, blue, and yellow over the cliffs. On any other night, it'd be the perfect recipe for a make out, but Brody's moves seem to have suddenly disappeared. He stares into his hands, looking more vulnerable than I've ever seen him.

I feel like a total jerk. I should never have mistrusted him. I reach over and lift his chin up so that he's facing me. "Brody, I'm so sorry. I should have believed you."

A firework pops in the distance. "How can I expect you to believe me? I haven't been totally honest with you since the day we met."

"You haven't?" My stomach drops as our car nears the top. The last thing I want to hear is that my brothers have been right all along.

"There are just some things going on in my life that I just can't tell you about. At least not right now."

I squirm, sliding back away from Brody. My imagination roams with the possibilities.

Brody reaches across the distance, placing his hand over mine. "But I want you to know this—training with you this summer—has meant a lot to me."

A smile begins to burst at the edges of my lips, but I squash it before it can fully take hold. "That's sweet of you to say, but . . ."

"But what?"

"But you still haven't told me what changed," I squeak. "Why you're here in California . . ."

"Abs, I want to tell you, but I can't get into it right now."

"You can't give me any clues?" I square my body, placing one hand on the lap bar.

Brody laughs so hard that it spreads to his eyes. "You really *are* persistent, aren't you?"

I look down at my feet. Strands of hair fall out of my ponytail.

"No, it's okay. It's one of the things I like most about you." He moves my hair behind my eyes. "Like I said when we were out on the boat, I have my priorities in line now. I didn't when I first met you."

*Ka-boom.* Another firework explodes, catching us both off guard.

"Did you see that?" Brody points to the descending remains of a fizzling blue firework.

I peer out, trying to get a better view just as we arrive at the wheel's highest point. The car sways and I fall across Brody's chest. He scoops me up with his arm.

I shudder—I shouldn't let him hold me. But then, before I know it, I've given in to the safety of his embrace. "So where do we go from here?" I whisper.

"Well, I'd like to keep training you for one," he says softly, running his free hand along my cheek.

"Okay . . ." I hesitate. "I think that can be arranged."

"And I'd like to kiss you. . . ."

I freeze up and try to extricate myself from Brody's grasp. If we were ever going to kiss again, now—with the pier below us and the stars above us—would be the time. But I can't let myself dive into that particular pool.

Brody pulls me back in one gentle but firm motion. "It's okay. I'm not going to try. I know how much your job means to you."

I relax against his chest.

"But promise me this: Forget that little deal we just made with the cars—you know, guessing the colors." He continues before I can insist that we didn't actually make a bargain. "How about this instead: if you win the competition, then you'll go to the Luau with me?"

"Are you serious? Another deal?" I exclaim. "That's like the fourth one you've tried to make with me in the last month."

"I'm desperate."

"Clearly. And don't go telling me again that it's just because I love games—"

Brody cuts me off. "Abs, I mean it. Think about what I'm saying."

I bite my lip. "That might not be the best idea."

"I know. I know. You're worried about your job—for this year, next year, and knowing you, probably also ten years in the future."

I giggle at that one.

He turns my head so I'm looking deep into his eyes. "But doesn't all that worrying get exhausting? Don't you ever just want to say what the heck?"

The breath sucks out of my lungs. I feel like I'm going to leave a puddle of myself on the car floor. "I can't," I say. "I *need* that scholarship. If I win it—*when* I win it—I can't risk the club's taking it away." With every ounce of restraint I can muster, I slide to the opposite side of the car, pulling my jacket tighter.

The car starts moving again.

Brody stares at me and bites his lip. "It's going to be one long summer, Abs."

I sit on my trembling hands. He has no idea.

# Chapter Twenty-One

**After an early morning** workout on the beach a few weeks later, I'm in the tower checking my assignment when Katie steps beside me.

"Looks like we're together again." Katie beams. She's dressed in full lifeguard gear—a fire engine red bathing suit, tank, and shorts—and gathers her short blonde hair into a small pony.

"I think it's safe to say that we're officially partners." I grin, thinking about how much I've learned from Katie over the last month and a half. I still haven't made a "real" save, but she's been pretty amazing about showing me the ropes.

"You're too cute," she says, squeezing out a glob of sunscreen onto her palm. She points to the orange sign next to the assignment sheet, the sunscreen bottle still in her hand. "So it says there that the currents are pulling people dangerously close to the cliffs today. We might have our first save of the season."

I read over the warning, mentally reviewing everything I've

learned about rips. "How will I know where the current is?" My heart pounds.

"I'll show you how to spot the current once we get out there," Katie says. "Remember, if a swimmer gets caught, tell them to relax. It only makes it worse if they swim against the current."

I nod intensely, trying to absorb everything Katie is saying.

"Don't be nervous. I'll meet you out there in a sec. Okay?"

Again, I nod.

"I just want to confirm the rest of this week's schedule with Denise." Katie leaves to track down Denise in her office.

I head to the exit, gnawing on my lip as I silently will Katie's meeting with Denise to be the fastest in history.

I descend the ramp to the beach and am met by a little girl with auburn pigtails. She's wearing a pink bathing suit with metallic embroidered stars. But unfortunately the silver stitching isn't nearly as noticeable as the tears that glisten in her eyes.

I squat in front of her so we're the same height. "Can I help you with something?"

She vigorously shakes her head no, swinging her pigtails back and forth. "I'm not allowed to talk to strangers." She sucks in a breath.

"I'm a lifeguard. I'm here to help you," I say. "See." I show her the lifeguard insignia on my bag.

She hiccups.

"How old are you?" I ask.

A fat tear rolls down her cheek.

"What's your favorite color?" I hope this will get her to open up.

"Pink," she says, whimpering.

"Oooh, I love pink! Just like your pretty bathing suit." I pause. "Did you lose your Mommy?"

The little girl nods.

"Okay . . ." I point to my bag again. "This says, 'lifeguard.' That means I'm here to help you find your mommy. It's my job."

I hold out my hand to her, standing up.

The little girl looks up at me and wipes her eyes with the backs of her hands. After a few seconds, she grabs my hand. "Okay."

I walk her back up the ramp. "We're going to go in the tower and find out where your mommy is." I hold the door open for her and discover that Brody has managed to squeeze by me while I was busy with the girl.

My heart leaps—the tension between us has practically been boiling over lately—but I ignore him for the time being.

"Here, sweetie." I point to a chair. "You can have a seat here." I wonder if Katie is still at the office with Denise or if she made it to the stand yet.

The girl sits down, holding her legs tight against her chest.

"Can you tell me your name?" I ask.

"Victoria," she whispers.

"And your last name?"

"Uh . . . Victoria Snyder Amy."

"Victoria Amy Snyder?" I gently correct her.

She nods.

"What's going on?" Brody murmurs to me.

"She lost her mom," I whisper, picking up the walkie-talkie from its holder resting on the wooden ledge.

"Aw . . . We'll find her," Brody says, pulling up a chair for himself.

I call the front desk to see if anyone has reported Victoria missing.

Meanwhile, Brody tries to comfort Victoria in my place. "Guess what?" he says, softening his voice.

Victoria's body stiffens like a board.

"I lost my mommy once . . ." Brody clears his throat. "I lost my mom when I was little too."

Victoria's eyes widen to the size of quarters. "You did?"

I look back and forth between Brody and Victoria; he really couldn't be handling her any better than he is. My heart melts like ice cream left out in the sun. Could he get any cuter?

"Yup. I lost her for ten really scary minutes. At a beach club. Just like you."

He looks up at me when he hears me confirming Victoria's story with her mom's at the front desk.

He mouths, "Is she there?"

I nod.

"You did?" Victoria inches closer to Brody.

Brody winks at me, breaking into a wide smile as he quickly turns back to Victoria. "Uh-huh. And just like you, she found me at the lifeguard tower."

"What?!" Victoria screeches just as a woman busts through the door.

She sprints across the room and scoops Victoria up into her arms. "There you are!"

The Beachwood Country Club manager follows behind her. He ignores me and walks directly over to Brody. "Way to go, son," he says, smacking Brody on the shoulder.

*He thinks Brody did this by himself?* My shoulders sink. I fumble for the door handle, a sudden case of claustrophobia overwhelming me.

And that's when I hear Brody stand up for me. "It was Abby Berkeley," he says, attempting to correct the manager's oversight. "She helped Victoria calm down and find her mom."

"Thanks, uh . . ." The manager glances down to check my nametag. Unfortunately for him, I'm not wearing one.

"Abby," I answer. He obviously wasn't paying attention. I nod at him and step outside to begin my shift.

**I head to the lifeguard stand,** barely able to control my inner fuming. I can't believe the manager just dodged me like that. My family would have a field day if they knew. I can already picture my brothers storming in with a baseball bat, ready to teach that manager a lesson for ignoring their little sister.

Not that I need their help.

I look over at the snack bar, scene of my imprisonment, and catch sight of the pool. I can't help but smile despite my frustration. Zoe is perched on a lifeguard chair. She's clearly attempting to watch the water, but two little girls won't stop badgering her.

I've been so involved with lifeguarding, training with Brody, and working the snack bar that I haven't had time to hang out with Zoe—or any of my other friends really—since that night at the pier. I wave at Zoe enthusiastically, but she barely nods in return, probably because between guarding the pool and entertaining the two girls clamoring for her attention, she's already maxed out.

I remind myself to text her before my snack bar shift to catch up. From the looks of it, I'd say she'll probably tell me that she's been babysitting. A lot.

"There you are . . ." Katie says as soon as she spots me at the lifeguard stand. "What took you so long?"

"Lost little girl," I say, pulling myself up on the seat.

"August is definitely the time of year for lost kids," she says, scanning the packed beach. "Kids have been on the beach for a couple of months. They get a little more brazen while their parents get a little more relaxed."

"How was your meeting with Denise?" I ask, hanging my bag over the seat.

"Fine. Quick." Katie is all business. She's obviously still concerned about today's water conditions.

"That's good." I pull out my whistle and adjust my sunglasses. When I look out at the ocean, two red flags flap in the rough wind. "And the rip currents?"

"Just a lot of whistling for people to move back in . . . Like right now." Katie stands up and blows her whistle, furiously waving her arms for a group of kids to move away from the cliffs and back to shore.

The scene reminds me of the talk we had on my first day—about how people get near the red flags even though they shouldn't.

"So you were gonna tell me about how to figure out where the rip current is." I shade my eyes from the sun. I can't seem to locate the signature backward wave we were told to keep an eye out for in training.

"See out there," Katie points to a section of water a few yards away from the cliffs. "That swirl is the rip current. That's what you want to avoid."

I look in the direction Katie's pointing, just barely making out the current, when I spot a group of boys tossing a football dangerously close to the flag.

"Urgh . . ." Katie says. She blows her whistle.

The boys don't move.

Katie grabs her buoy. "Don't those morons see the flags?"

"Can I go?" I'm eager to get some real in-the-water experience.

Katie skims her foot along the edge of the stand. "I don't know. You have no experience with rip currents. They can be tricky even for an experienced lifeguard."

"I can do it." I tear off my shades and grab my buoy.

"Okay. Just stay away from the rip. Move the boys and get out. I'll be right behind you," Katie says, talking into the two-way radio.

I jump from the stand. *This is it.* The day I make a name for myself. I jog into the shallow surf, my heart pounding. The water splashes against my shins.

I surface dive into a waist-high wave, reminding myself to swim *with* the current, not against it, if I get caught.

I emerge from the wave and spot the boys. They're tossing a football directly in front of me, oblivious to the current. All it would take is a couple of steps backward and the boy farthest out would be instantly pulled under. I have to act now.

"Excuse me," I say, trying to get their attention. The undertow pulls me back a step.

The boy next to me dives to catch the football. He does a belly flop into a wave, splashing me in the face. To his great pleasure, he manages to retrieve the football.

I decide that now is as good a time as any to make my big entrance. "Please either return to shore or swim away from the flag. We're keeping bathers close to shore today."

"Nah, I don't think we're going to do that. Thanks for the advice, though," says the boy who threw the football. He turns to the guy who caught it. "Hey, Jonah! Doesn't she look like that girl from *Baywatch*. Not the one with the big boobs, the other one."

"Oh, yeah. I know who you mean. My dad was, like, in love with her. Nicole Egg or something." The boy standing next to me— Jonah, apparently—squints. "Don't you work at the snack bar?"

I lose my balance for a moment, the undertow pulling me to the right. "It's very important that you listen to me about the current. It can be very dangerous. Please make your way to the sand."

"Save me, Snack Girl—I'm drowning." A third boy smacks the water with his hands, pretending to be sucked down into the water.

I hear a splash behind me.

"Is there a problem?" Katie asks. Her voice is more severe than I've ever heard it.

"We're just having a little fun," the boy who threw the football says, his voice taking on an apologetic tone that wasn't there before.

"You better not be giving Abby a hard time, Todd," she says sternly, glaring at the boy.

"No. Wouldn't dream of it." Todd holds his hands up like he's about to get arrested.

"Good. Exactly what I want to hear."

The water pulls me again. I take a few steps toward Katie.

"This is a dangerous situation today," Katie reiterates to the boys. "You need to move."

The group of them finally begin to trudge back to shore. They don't seem happy about it.

Katie turns her attention to me. "Abby, please return to the bench to watch the other swimmers." She purses her lips.

"I can handle . . ."

"Please."

I clear my throat so I don't cry. I charge roughly ahead through the water and squeeze my buoy handle. I don't know how I've been managing to kid myself this last month, thinking that the club might accept me as one of their own if I win the scholarship. Between Brody getting credit for helping that little girl and now this, I'm starting to feel like this place will never see me as anything more than a charity case, as the snack bar girl who they "let" lifeguard because Brody Wilson made a special request. I kick the sand as I make my way back to my assigned spot.

Brody is there when I reach the stand.

"What was that all about?" he asks, reaching out a hand to comfort me.

"I don't want to talk about it." I pull away from him and begin my climb back up the chair.

"Not your day, is it?" He jokes.

I grimace. "Not my summer." I throw my buoy down, not bothering to check whether I've managed to hang it correctly.

"Don't let those boys bother you," Brody says, plopping himself next to me. "They've probably had a huge crush on you all summer."

"I don't think so. . . ." I wrap my towel around me and let out a sigh. All this work for nothing. What lifeguard can't even move swimmers?

Brody kneels down and begins gently rubbing my wet foot. "Abs, I know you want to be the best."

I move my foot away from his touch. "We're at the club," I say through clenched teeth.

He pushes himself back up, clearly deliberating about how best to deal with me. He ultimately goes with teacherly advice. "You're a new guard. You can't expect to be the best your first summer. It takes time to learn how to be a good lifeguard and—"

I cut him off. "Thanks for the pep talk."

Brody continues where he left off. "And it takes time to learn how to deal with the members."

I look up at him. I'm fairly sure my disappointment has reached my eyes. "I can't even get some kids to move."

"Don't take it so hard," Brody urges, placing his hand onto my shoulder.

I shudder, shaking his hand off. Brody Wilson is the *prince* of Beachwood; he can't even begin to understand how I feel. I was right to dodge his invite to the Luau. My conviction that I won't be able to attend—with or without him—was renewed the moment the manager walked into that tower. And the boys' refusal to listen just confirmed it.

A shrill voice calls out, "Is there a problem?"—the same question that Katie just asked those guys by the cliffs. Except the woman before me is definitely *not* Katie.

"No. No problem, Denise," I answer, as chastened as the boys were just a few minutes ago. *There will be a problem when you find out Brody and I hang out every day after our shift.*

I look out at the water again. My stomach is in my throat.

Katie jogs up to us, holding the football. "No problem," she echoes. "Abby is doing an amazing job."

"That's what I like to hear, Berkeley," Denise says, grinning proudly. Brody and I can be seen in the reflection of her wrap-around sunglasses. We both look like we're crawling out of our skin.

Denise continues. "I stopped by to remind you that the sign-up sheet for the Last Blast Competition will be posted outside the snack bar tomorrow morning. I hope you're participating this year. It's going to be a great event."

"Wouldn't miss it," I say, keeping my eyes on Denise's supervisor's jacket and off Brody.

"Fabulous. I think you're going to be one of the favorites to win." Denise pulls out her radio. "Now get back to work." She walks briskly toward the tower.

My mood lifts for the first time today. Denise sees me as a *lifeguard*. She wants me to compete. And after I win the scholarship, the rest of the club will follow her lead. They'll have to.

Brody taps my foot with his buoy. "See? That has to make you feel better," he whispers.

I exhale, allowing Denise's encouragement to wash over me.

"So I'll see you later tonight for training?" Brody asks. The twinkle in his eye tells me that he has more than just training on his mind.

I nod, staring at the water. I'm grateful that he doesn't bring up the Luau again. One thing at a time . . .

Katie climbs back on the stand as Brody walks away. "What was that all about?" she asks.

*What? Does she mean me and Brody? The way he was talking to me?* I turn my head right and left, frantic that Denise saw the way Brody and I left things, that she'll realize something's been going on between us—even if it's only training. I can't let everything fall apart now, not when I'm so close to winning the scholarship—and maybe something more.

That's when I make eye contact with another unwelcome voyeur. Lexi. She nods at me, raising her left eyebrow. She's seen. *She knows.*

She jogs up to join Brody as he makes his way to the tower.

# Chapter Twenty-Two

**Thanks to my morning shift** at the snack bar, I'm the first in line at the Last Blast Competition sign-up sheet the next morning. Who knew all those hours at Sunset would be good for something? My insides twist as I sign my name next to the number-one spot—whether it's due to excitement about the competition or anxiety about what Lexi's going to do with her big discovery, it's too early to tell.

"There you are!" Zoe calls out. I'm shocked to see her at this hour.

"Zoe!" I yell, holding out my arms for a hug. "What are you doing here this early?"

"Signing up for the competition. Duh." She doesn't hug me. "I was worried that Denise would have an epiphany and only allow beach guards or something."

"That sounds like exactly the sort of thing she'd do." I adjust my ponytail, feeling surprisingly uncomfortable around my best friend.

She grabs the pen from my hand and quickly signs her name under mine. "So I haven't seen you in forever, Abby Cadabby."

"I know! Not since that night at the pier."

"Speaking of which, I wanted to tell you about that girl we saw, the one that Brody was with." She twirls the pen around her finger by the attached string.

"Oh, don't worry about it. I know all about her." I look around, surprised that we're still the only lifeguards here. With everything I've heard about the competition, I'd think that people would storm the snack bar to get their names on that list.

"You do?" She stops twirling her finger. The pen hangs there.

"Yeah. Turns out she's Brody's sister." I eye Zoe curiously. Why are we even talking about this?

"So I've heard. But Kylie and Missy told me that—"

I cut her off. "Zoe, I'm really thrilled to see you, but Brody and I are kind of in a reasonably okay place, and I don't want a turn in the Kylie-and-Missy rumor mill to ruin that."

"Fine." She crosses her arms, still holding on to the pen for dear life. "So what have you been up to lately?"

"Oh, training, lifeguarding, training, working at the snack bar, training." I giggle, trying to lighten the mood.

"That's a lot of training," Zoe deadpans.

"I really want to win that scholarship."

"Shocker." She holds the pen by the attached string and hangs it back around the pushpin.

"It's not just for me, you know?" I play with the pushpin.

"It isn't?"

I push the pin in hard and face Zoe head-on. "Don't you want

177

to catch the look on Lexi's face when something finally doesn't go her way?"

"Now that I'd pay to see." She beams. It seems as if we're finally connecting again. "So I guess you're too busy to come to the bonfire then?" she asks, a hint of sarcasm in her voice.

So much for connecting.

"What bonfire?" I ask, crossing my arms.

"Uh. Just the biggest party of the summer." Zoe looks at me like I've swallowed a little too much saltwater.

"I thought Last Blast was the biggest party of the summer. . . ."

"Okay, so this is second only to that."

"What makes it second?"

"It's only for lifeguards." She pauses, catching sight of Jason who's just arrived at the snack bar. "But a lot of times people try to bring a few friends from the club anyway."

I nod at Jason, wondering whether he'd be the kind of "friend" the other lifeguards would want at their bonfire.

"Are you bringing anyone?" I ask.

"Yeah, I thought I'd see if Kylie and Missy want to come."

I narrow my eyes, surprised that Kylie and Missy are at the top of Zoe's list. What *has* she been doing in my absence?

"Anyway, people get together on Saturday night at a secluded beach that's only accessible during low tide. There's a DJ and a bonfire and food and drinks."

"Nobody told me."

Zoe rolls her eyes. "Maybe that's because you've gone off the grid."

"I've just been working and training a lot."

"I know. You mentioned that. That's why I've stopped asking you to come babysit with me." She waits for my reaction.

I'm at a loss.

"Or haven't you noticed?"

"I had. And I wanted to ask you—"

"Surprise. Surprise. Look who it is." Lexi sneers, interrupting my attempt to fix things with Zoe.

"You got me," I say, my stomach dropping. Is Lexi going to spill the beans now or wait for the perfect moment?

"Should have known that Abby Berkeley would be the first to sign up for the Last Blast Competition." Lexi pushes in front of us, grabbing the pen.

"Obviously," Zoe mutters under her breath. Then she switches to her normal voice. "Okay, girls, I gotta go. Some of us have to babysit." She takes off toward the playground to greet a mom and her twins waiting by the swings.

I turn back to Lexi. "How are you on this gorgeous August day?"

"I'm fine. But it's you I'm worried about, Snack Girl. You're juggling an awful lot this summer, don't you think?"

*I can't kill her now*, I tell myself. *I've got to save it for the competition.* "I don't know what you're talking about." I plop my bag on a stool.

I feel Jason's eyes on us as he hangs some glasses.

"Well . . ." Lexi trails the edge of the granite countertop with the tip of her index finger. "You know. It must be hard trying to keep all your secrets in order."

"Yeah. Sure. I guess," I say, trying to maintain a calm exterior. Meanwhile, my mind races: Is this it? Is this the moment she tells me that she's going to rat me out?

"Hey, Mr. Murphy," I hear Jason say to my left. I glance in his direction and discover that Zoe's dad has just sat down at the bar. Big surprise.

"Early bird today?" Jason asks.

"Rough night," Zoe's dad grumbles. "Give me my usual."

Lexi continues, ignoring the scene unfolding beside us. "Lifeguarding shifts, working the snack bar, training for the competition—must be tough."

*How long is she going to make me suffer before she just comes out with it already?*

"Don't you think it's a bit early for a Jack and Coke?" Jason asks. I can't seem to tune out their conversation. "How about a little OJ?" he suggests.

"Just give me my usual," Mr. Murphy growls.

Jason sets a glass down.

Lexi smirks, drawing me away from Jason's attempts to convince Mr. Murphy of the benefits of Vitamin C. "I hear you've been working with one trainer in particular," she taunts.

Wow. And here I thought that Lexi just *saw* me with Brody and interpreted accordingly. Apparently, she heard our entire conversation.

*Unless he told her . . .*

I steel my nerves, refusing to let myself be bullied. "Why? Are you looking for a new trainer?"

Lexi sniggers. "Oh, you're good, Abby Berkeley. But you and I both know that I've already met the trainer I'm talking about. In fact, I've known him my whole life."

"That must be why your shoulders are so cut. What exercises do you—"

"Cut the BS, Abby. I know you're training with Brody."

I freeze.

"What's wrong? Didn't know I knew, huh?"

I swallow, pulling my apron out of my bag.

"Yup. I know all about your little late nights at Brody's house. I guess Brody forgot to mention to you that we have a *long* history. Did you know my weekend home is only a few doors down from his in the Colony?"

*Why didn't he tell me?*

"Kind of made it convenient when we used to be together. All those hot summer nights on the beach. Good thing we didn't have to worry about rules back then. But then again, I don't think we could have kept our hands off each other."

My fists clench. I *knew* there was still something between them.

*Clang. Pshhh . . .* Glass shatters. I look over to see that Jason has dropped a bottle of whiskey.

Hmm . . . he's not usually that clumsy.

"One more," Mr. Murphy taps his knuckles on the bar, his Rolex watch banging against the counter. Obviously, *our* conversation is of no concern to him.

Lexi looks visibly startled, but she continues laying into me. "Where do you live, Abs? That is what Brody lovingly calls you, right?"

I glare at Lexi, wondering what she'd do if I threw Mr. Murphy's drink in her face.

She continues with her ambush, blissfully unaware of my covert impulses. "Do you live in one of those rundown old houses? I'm betting that you do. . . ."

"Shut up, Lexi," I say, shaking out my apron.

Mr. Murphy stumbles to his feet and heads toward the beach. He grabs a discarded pair of goggles as if he plans to go for a swim.

At least Zoe is off babysitting. . . .

"I'm just here to warn you. That's all," Lexi says innocently. "If it was so easy for me to find out about you and Brody, then it's probably pretty simple for everyone else. You guys might want to be a little more discreet when you're sneaking around."

My mouth is dry. Sweat beads on my back. Does that mean she's *not* going to tell Denise?

"We're just training," I say, tying my apron strings behind me.

"Whatever. You're just lucky I don't turn you in."

*Wait, what?!* Is she seriously going to keep my secret. She must be after something. I look Lexi in the eye. "What do you want?"

She cackles. "To warn you that you and Brody are just a summer thing. There's no way that whatever's going on between you two will last."

"Yeah? How can you be so sure?" It must be that she intends to put an end to me and Brody—not that there really is a "me and Brody"—so that she can have him all to herself.

Jason picks up a towel and begins wiping the counter furiously.

"Brody is from a certain breed. Pure. Not a mutt if you get where I'm going with this."

I roll my eyes. "We're not dogs, Lexi."

"Thanks for the science lesson, Abs." She puts the emphasis on my name. "What you don't understand—what you can *never* understand—is that we've been trained to act a certain way."

"So you're a robot then?"

"Robots aren't trained." Lexi furrows her brow, then regains her composure. "We've all been through cotillion, you know. Plus, club events, charity balls, fundraisers. Do you even know what any of that entails?"

"Are you done yet?" I sigh.

Lexi continues. "What have you trained for? Cleaning up after people?"

Jason throws down his towel. "Enough, Lexi!" he screams. "Enough!" He stands between us. "Abby here doesn't want to hear about your warped sense of the world. So why don't you just go and direct your venom at someone who cares."

Lexi's face turns red. She looks genuinely mortified. "Jason, I . . ." she stammers.

"Go," he says, stone-faced.

She turns around and tramps out of the snack bar, her expression far guiltier than the one worn by the boys Katie rounded up yesterday.

I look from her back to Jason.

What just happened?

# Chapter Twenty-Three

**"Mr. Murphy!"** I exclaim as soon as Lexi is out of earshot.

"What?" Jason asks, barely paying attention. His mind is clearly elsewhere.

"He grabbed a pair of goggles. And it looked like he was going to the beach!" I frantically untie my apron and rip off my work shirt. Good thing I decided to wear my bathing suit under my snack bar uniform today.

"Oh no!" Jason shouts.

"I was so caught up in everything Lexi was saying that all I thought about was how it was good that Zoe wouldn't see her dad embarrass himself." I step out of my shorts, tripping on them as I look up at the clock. "But the lifeguards aren't on duty till ten. How much did he have to drink?

Jason motions to four empty glasses—two Jack and cokes and two shots. "All in fifteen minutes."

"Okay, you go to the tower to call this in. I'll go see if I can spot Mr. Murphy." I run out before Jason can protest.

I can't decide whether it's good or bad that Lilly wasn't here to see this. I doubt she would have been able to stop Mr. Murphy from drinking—he *is* a member after all—but maybe she would have known what to do.

I grab a buoy from the side of the lifeguard stand and dash across the sand. I scan the ocean. It's empty. No swimmers. No victim. Nobody struggling.

Thank God. Mr. Murphy decided he was too drunk to swim.

Jason scampers over to me. "I radioed in an intoxicated swimmer," he says, out of breath. "Denise told me that she was fifteen minutes away and that you should try to talk him out of the water."

"He's not here," I reply.

"What?" Jason looks right and left, searching the water alongside me.

"I don't see him," I say, oddly calm.

The tranquility doesn't last.

"Abby look! He just went under!" Jason yells, pointing to an area beyond the cliffs.

My instincts take over. "Call 911!" I shout, already sprinting to the water.

My lungs burn as I dive under a wave with my buoy in hand. I swim as fast as I can to where Mr. Murphy was last sighted, ignoring the stinging of the saltwater as it assaults my eyes. When the bubbles clear, I make out a dark shadow up ahead.

I plunge back into the water and swim faster and faster, harnessing everything I learned in training. I pop my head out for a breath and am bashed by a wave, but this time I can definitely make out a figure flailing about helplessly. I dip back underneath and push myself. *It's Zoe's dad!* my mind screams. I come up again for air and can just about grab one of Mr. Murphy's waving arms.

I swim underwater and around Mr. Murphy. I grab him underneath his arms, using my feet to push off the bottom and propel us upward.

Mr. Murphy fights me as we rise to the surface. His arms thrash and he kicks me hard in my recently healed knee.

Pain radiates from my knee to my foot. I let go of him. He dips underneath the surface.

Tears fill my eyes and then, as if out of a dream, Katie appears in the distance, pushing the paddleboat into the water. I signal to her that I need assistance.

Unfortunately, though, I can't wait for her arrival. Mr. Murphy is in trouble right now. I inhale, forcing myself to ignore the ache in my knee, and dive back under. I wrap my arms around Mr. Murphy's chest and attempt to kick my legs. But Mr. Murphy is too heavy to move.

I pop my head up and see that Zoe's father is still fighting the water.

"Please relax," I plead with him, tossing him my buoy. "It's going to be all right."

He's back underwater before he can hear me—or grab on.

"Where is he?!" Katie shouts as she arrives next to us in the boat.

I point, swallowing a lump in my throat. *I can't let Zoe's dad drown. Not on my watch.*

"Pull him to the surface so he can grab the paddle." She holds out the oar.

"He's fighting," I say, feeling the panic rise in my throat.

"Just do it!"

I suck in a big gulp of air and plunge back beneath the surface. I don't let myself be held back by the burning in my eyes—or in my knee. I wrap my arms around Mr. Murphy's chest. He thrashes and I'm barely able to hold on to my loose grip. Using my good foot, I push on the sea bottom.

It's just enough to get us to the surface for a second.

He breathes and thrashes. I have to let go or I'm going down with him.

I come up for a burst of air and then dive underwater. This time, Katie joins me. Bubbles surround us as we wrap our arms around Mr. Murphy's trunk. She holds up one finger and we both push on the sea floor. This time, we're able to pull Zoe's father to the surface. He grabs the buoy.

Adrenaline kicks in once I resurface. *I have to get him to the shore.* I maneuver the buoy in front of his chest.

"I got him!" I shout to Katie.

"I'm in front," she yells, pulling us to shore.

I scissor kick, using the waves to propel us.

*I can do this,* I think.

That is until Mr. Murphy begins to choke. He waves his arms in a misguided attempt to clear his throat.

"Please calm down," I say. "Everything is going to be all right."

Mr. Murphy finally relaxes into my arms. I can't tell if he's just stopped fighting or if he's passed out.

"Hold on, Mr. Murphy. We're almost to the sand," Katie shouts.

We ride another wave into shore.

*Splash.* This one pushes us to shallow water.

"We're on sand," I say once my feet hit the bottom.

"The ambulance is on its way!" Jason yells, running toward us.

"I don'th needth no Godth damnsh ambulancesh," Mr. Murphy slurs. He wiggles out of my grasp.

"Mr. Murphy. I don't think it's a good idea for you to walk unassisted. You're probably very tired from your struggle," Katie says.

Before I can catch him, Mr. Murphy falls face first into the ankle-deep water.

"Mr. Murphy!" I yell, dropping down next to him.

I gently roll him to his side. He thanks me by vomiting all over the sand.

"Make sure his airway is clear!" Katie dictates.

Zoe's dad moans as I listen for breathing.

"You're going to be fine, Mr. Murphy. Just sit tight until help arrives." The waves begin to wash away the vomit.

I turn to Jason. "Can you grab us some warm towels?"

Jason dashes toward the lobby.

Mr. Murphy rolls over. "Where am I?"

I look around for help. In the distance, I see Denise sprinting over. "You're at the beach club. You've had too much to drink this morning and you went for a swim. You're going to be okay."

A siren screeches. Flashing lights spill from the lobby.

"Huh?" He squints.

Jason returns with the towels.

"Thanks." I grab the towels and lay them across Mr. Murphy to keep him warm. He starts to drift off to sleep.

"What happened?" Denise yells.

"Abby and Katie saved Mr. Murphy's life," Jason explains, patting me on the back. I cough out the water still lodged in my throat pipes.

Finally, the paramedics take over and Denise relaxes. The danger has passed. "Nice job, girls," she says. Her voice is a mixture of intense pride at our having saved a man in her absence and overwhelming relief—there will be no lawsuits today.

"Thanks," I squeak, attempting to catch my breath. I watch the paramedics as they transport Mr. Murphy into the ambulance.

Denise motions that we're free to go.

I tremble as I walk across the pathway to the snack bar—I still have an hour left of my shift. It's no exaggeration to say that literally every part of my body quivers—my legs, my lips, my arms, my hands. The shaking doesn't stop until I feel a warm body press into me. Muscular arms wrap around my frame and a familiar musky scent drifts into my nostrils.

"Brody," I gasp.

"I just heard what happened." He sounds out of breath. "Are you okay?"

"I uh . . ." I disentangle myself from him and pick my apron up from where I left it on the counter. My hands are still unsteady. Hot tears push against me eyes. "I'll be . . ."

Brody lays his hand on my shoulder. "You need to go home," he says. "Lilly would never expect you to work after this."

I drop the apron on the counter. *Lilly!* My mind sounds a warning bell. I look around—she's still not here. Fortunately, neither are any customers. I guess they must have seen that no one was serving and left. "People are gonna complain," I say nonsensically.

Brody glances around. "No one's here," he whispers. "No one but you and me."

I look up into Brody's eyes. There's pity there—and something else. "The sheet—Lexi—Zoe's dad," I say gravely. I can tell I'm not making any sense.

"Abby, I think you should go home." Brody moves a piece of hair out of my eyes.

"But I have to call Zoe. Tell her what happened. And what about Lilly . . ." She should be here any minute.

A single tear drips onto the counter.

"Zoe will understand." He runs his fingers through my hair. "And don't worry about the snack bar. Jason can handle it."

I sniffle and Brody must take this for an invitation because he wraps his arms around me once more.

I let him envelop me, fortifying myself in his embrace.

But then I tense up. "We're at the club," I screech.

"No one is paying attention, Abs. Everyone is busy with the save."

I look around. He's right.

He guides me out of the club and into his Jeep.

# Chapter Twenty-Four

**"Is this it?"** I stare across the Pacific Coast Highway to the top of an enormous copper-colored cliff. Beyond the brush, the sun sets over the rolling water.

"Yup." Brody slows down. Cars whiz by as he attempts to parallel park. "Ready to do some hiking?"

"Hiking?" I ask, quickly sending Zoe another text. Still no reply after at least eight messages. That's weird. I've been calling her since I saved her father and nothing. She must be really freaked out.

"Hiking? I wore flip-flops," I say to Brody as he climbs out of his Jeep.

After the big save, Brody took me to his house—I managed to be coherent enough to recognize what would happen if he came to mine—and we relaxed by the pool. At first, I just cried. And Brody held me. And then we talked, really talked. It was the first time since the swim meet that we had a real, uninterrupted conversation—no accusations, no worrying about why Brody withdrew from Michigan, and no swimming laps. He shared the story of his first save and how it took him a couple of days to let it sink in. Eventually, I stopped shaking. At one point, I even opened my eyes to discover that I'd calmed down enough to fall asleep.

Brody opens the passenger door. "Thanks," I say as I climb out of the car. My stomach does flip-flops. Even after all the time Brody and I spent together, I don't know if it was a good idea to come with him to the bonfire. Part of me thinks that I shouldn't have even come here at all.

He grabs my hand and the enormity of what would happen if someone saw us rushes back to me. I can't let Brody think that just because we shared the most wonderful afternoon, we're suddenly together. There's still the scholarship to think about. And my family. Not to mention whatever Lexi has in store—I can't imagine that she plans to stop at a mere warning.

"What are you doing?" I ask, feeling queasy about rocking the boat.

"You agreed to come to this together so I figure we're officially out of the closet." He looks both ways before pulling me behind him as he crosses the street.

"Not exactly." I shove my phone into the back pocket of my cut-offs. "I figured this was more of a *Look they showed up at the same time* kind of thing—you know, *What a coincidence!*—than a *Look they came together* kind of thing." I pull my hand back from his. "And I just don't think it's a good idea to hold hands next to the busiest road in Malibu."

Brody lets out a sigh. "Are you ever going to stop caring about what people think?" He looks up at the darkening sky.

"It's not just that I care what people think." I stamp off, then turn back around. "It's that I've put too much into training to blow it two weeks before the competition." I wave my hands, exasperated, then take off across the highway.

Brody shakes his head and follows me.

When I reach the cliff, I glance over at the dense brush. I can't figure out how we're going to get to the other side of the cliff without some serious rock climbing equipment. "Where is this bonfire anyway?"

Brody waves me over. "Follow me."

I trail behind him through the brush and onto a narrow path. I gingerly peek over the edge and spot waves splashing against the jagged rocks below. Talk about a long fall. I swiftly shift my body weight back to solid ground. "I don't see any steps," I say.

"Over here." Brody walks perilously close to the edge.

I tremble for a second at the thought of something happening to him. I should be used to the landscape—I grew up in Malibu after all—but this cliff is seriously steep.

Brody peeks over the side and I seize up. "Ready for a workout?" he asks, a glint in his eye.

"What?" I come around to join him and see how he intends for us to make our escape. "There's no way . . ." I stare at what must be the steepest, skinniest staircase I've ever seen. It looks like one thousand steps. "Look at the rust. I don't think it can hold us."

"I thought you were tough," Brody begins to scale the steps two at a time, launching off the railing like it's a ski pole.

"I *am* tough. I just don't have a death wish." I walk down the steps gingerly, never descending more than one at a time. I call out to Brody, who's already yards beyond me. "I've never been anywhere near this beach. Sure it's not private?"

"Positive. There's not a house near this place."

"Why hold the bonfire in such an obscure spot?" I ask, gripping the railing as tightly as I can. A flowering cactus brushes up against my bare leg.

"It's a tradition. That way no one from the club can come unless a guard invites them."

"Do any non-guards even come to this?" I pick up some steam, comfortable in the knowledge that I'm not about to plunge to my death.

"Not really. Just a few girls who can't stand to miss out on anything."

That's good. At least now I feel a little bit less guilty that I let my fears that Jason wouldn't make the cut with the other guards stop me from inviting him.

Brody reaches the last step and propels himself feet first over the railing. I reach the end a few minutes later and am quickly whisked into Brody's arms. He gently lowers me to the cool sand. For a second, I stare into his eyes. Then he leans toward me until our lips are only inches apart.

My heart races. We haven't kissed since the swim meet, and with good reason—once we start, I don't know if I'll be able to stop.

I can't help it. I turn my head side to side to see if anyone is watching us. Unless boulders have eyes, it seems that we're in the clear. But still, I don't know if I can do this—at least not before the competition.

Brody quickly sizes up my nervousness. "How about just me

194

and you hang out for a bit before we join the others?" he plays with the tip of my ponytail.

"But what about . . ." I bite my bottom lip.

"Shhh . . ." He holds one finger up in front of his lips, then bends it, motioning for me to follow him. "No more worries from you." He reaches out his hand and I take it. It's rough from the months Brody has spent out in the sun, but it calms me more than the softest blanket.

Cool ocean water splashes our feet as Brody pulls me around the base of a large tan cliff. We reach the other side and I discover that Brody has brought me to a tiny cove. I toss off my flip-flops and plop down on the warm sand, stretching out my legs so that the surf runs over my toes. Brody does the same next to me. Washed-up kelp and tiny rocks frame our little private paradise.

It's all so serene that I can almost forget the horror I felt this morning, watching Zoe's dad struggle to keep his head above water. Part of me knows that there are probably still other horrors in store—Lexi ratting me out for one—but for now it seems as if things might just work out. That is, if Brody ever actually tells me the truth about why he's in California this summer.

"I never get tired of staring at the ocean," Brody muses, gazing at the waves crashing against the rocks. As the water spills toward us, he stretches out on his side next to me.

I shut my eyes for a second and breathe in slowly. "So, is that why we're here? To talk about the ocean?"

"That and other things." Brody draws circles on my knee with his index finger. His touch is soft, steady, and ever so slightly ticklish. It sends goose bumps up and down my legs.

I look into his magnetic green eyes—I could swim forever in those eyes—and my heart beats a mile a minute. Then my palms start sweating and shivers run down my spine; it feels as if I'm about to hyperventilate. "You have to tell me!" I scream.

I throw my hand over my mouth, covering it completely.

"Uh . . . okay," says Brody, totally bewildered by my behavior. "What do you want to hear?"

"I, um, want to know . . ." I clear my throat, still shocked by my outburst. "Can you look away from me, at the ocean?"

"Why?"

"Just please."

He smirks and looks out at the horizon.

"Okay, I didn't mean to yell, Brody, but here's the deal. I'm really confused. And I have been for, like, forever. Or at least the last month and a half. I know that we're training and everything, but you keep hinting that you want more. You even invited me to the Luau. And that's definitely a date thing."

"More than once," he grumbles.

"Yes, exactly. You even tried to make the invites into a kind of game. And I don't get it. You're starting college in a couple of weeks, I've never met your parents, and you and Lexi seem to have something going on that I definitely don't want to get in the middle of. Plus, you never really told me what changed—why you're here, I mean. And don't tell me about how you just want to stay local and take classes at UCLA or whatever. That's not a reason."

"It's not?" Brody looks back at me.

"It's not. Turn around."

He obliges, grinning to himself.

"So, anyway, you never told me why you made this big, life-altering decision. And I have to think that it was because of something really, really bad. Or because you're secretly in love with Lexi. And I get that I never really pushed it much, but that's only because I never let myself think that we could have a future together. You know, because of the club rule and everything. And this whole time I wanted to believe that it didn't matter, but now it does matter and . . ." I stop my diatribe mid-breath and wait for Brody to say something.

He doesn't. He continues looking out to the horizon, his eyes glazing over.

"Look, Brody, really there's no hard feelings. If you want to hook up with college girls, fine. If you want to run back to Lexi, fine. If you two are already together and you're just using me as a diversion, that's fine too. Just be honest with me. Do you have some kind of master plan or are you just looking to get with as many girls as possible?"

"Is that what you still think this is?"

He glances at me and I look away. I can't bear to see his expression. "That's the thing, Brody. I don't know what this is. Or even what I want it to be. At first you said that you didn't want to be with me because of college. But you're still going to college, even if you're not going to Michigan. You start, like, next week or something."

"Yeah so?"

"So you'll do your thing and eventually settle down with a pure-bred rich girl who knows how to walk and talk at parties."

"Huh?"

"I'm a mutt." I stand up and begin to pace. I don't want Brody to see that my eyes have begun to fill with tears.

"Like a dog?"

"Yeah." I wipe a tear away with the back of my hand.

"Why would you think that?"

"Don't you get it? I'm not like you and the rest of your friends. I work at the freaking snack bar." I sniffle. "Just go. I understand. I'll have my brother or dad pick me up. They'll be more than happy to."

Brody grabs hold of my arm just like he did that first day after the lifeguard meeting. "I don't want to go."

I turn my back to Brody. I can't stop the tears from falling. But I don't have to look Brody in the eye as it happens.

"Abby, who gave you the idea that we can all be divided into different kinds of dogs?"

"Your friend," I mumble. "Lexi."

"And you believed her?"

"She's known you your whole life." Another tear escapes. I wipe it away.

"Well then, clearly that doesn't mean anything."

"It meant enough that you two dated." I sniffle.

"We dated because her dad and my dad are business partners. It was expected of us. But sometimes it's the things we least expect that are the most exciting."

"Brody, what are you saying?" I look back at him.

Brody visibly pains at the sight of my tear-stained cheeks. Then he takes a deep breath. "It's about time that I let you in on what's really going on." He squeezes my hand. I try to pull away. He doesn't let me.

"I should have told you all this a long time ago. It's about my mom."

"Look, Brody, you don't have to . . ." A wave crashes into the beach.

"She has cancer."

"Oh my God, Brody." I let go of his hand and wrap my arms around his thick shoulders, squeezing as hard as I can.

After a few minutes, Brody gently pulls away from me. "It feels so good to finally tell someone."

I pull him down on the sand with me. Then I begin to massage his back.

"My mom . . ." He stops, staring at the sand. "I just . . . I couldn't tell a lot of people what's going on at my house."

I slide my hand underneath his T-shirt, rubbing his bare skin.

"Believe me, Abs. I wanted to. And I wanted you to meet her. And my dad and my sister. I wanted to invite you inside my house. But I just couldn't."

Lexi. She must have known all along. She knew Brody would never invite me inside because of his mom and she used that to plant doubt in my mind about Brody. *I'm going to kill her.*

"Her disease is a secret. See, if people find out she's sick, it will set off a panic with her clients. Don't ask me to explain the details. Not sure I even understand it all. All I know is she's holed up in the house fighting this disease. And we can't tell anyone." He pauses, catching his breath. "That's why I came back—I'm all she's got." His expression grows even more pained. "And you know she and Mara have hardly spoken in the last few years, and . . ."

I place my finger in front of his lips. "Shh . . . You don't have to explain." I look at him with new eyes. "You're amazing."

"I'm not." Brody tenses up.

"No, you are. You know how few people would have given up swimming at Michigan so that they could be there for their parents?"

"Nah, anyone would have done the same thing. I couldn't just up and leave when my mom was suffering like that."

"So why did you decide to come back to the club?"

"After my mom gave up on trying to convince me to go to Michigan, she thought it was best if I kept things as normal as possible." He pauses. "When Denise heard I was going to be around, she called me in to get all of my paperwork set up. And that's when I saw your name in the pile of lifeguarding apps."

"And so you recommended me for the job." I finish his thought.

"Yeah, I thought that at least one good thing should come out of all this misery. It felt kind of like fate? You know?"

"Yeah," I say, pushing back my remaining tears.

"And you know what else is fate?" Brody looks into my eyes, squeezing my hand.

"What?" I sniffle.

"That I'm going to kiss you now."

His lips brush against mine, hesitantly at first. Shivers run down my spine and I silently beg him to go further than the few pecks he gave me in May. We must have some kind of telepathic connection because it's as if he hears my thoughts. He dives into my mouth, moving deeper and deeper until our tongues find a rhythm. His mouth is warm and he smells like the sea.

And I'm officially in heaven.

# Chapter Twenty-Five

**I lie back against** Brody's chest, my heart still aflutter. I can barely manage to pay attention to his telling me about the vacation he took over spring break—I'm still so caught up in how unbelievable it felt to have his lips pressed against mine again after all this time. So caught up, in fact, that I can't remember why I waited so long.

"You took a cruise?" I eventually echo. I've lost track of time—I don't know whether we were kissing for hours or mere moments.

"Yup," he says, all nonchalant.

I stop mentally replaying what just happened between us long enough to focus on what he's saying. I guess in Brody's world, a cruise around the Hawaiian islands is no big deal. "What was it like?" I ask.

"I don't know. The usual."

"What's the usual?"

"You know, we stopped at a few islands."

"And that was just your spring break trip?"

"Yeah. Where did you go?"

"Uh . . . Home." I say, pulling my sweatshirt sleeves down over my hands.

"How about winter break?"

"Let me think about this," I hold my finger to my cheek, pretending to be deep in thought. "Home." I pause. "How about you?"

"We go skiing in Aspen during the winter. We would have gone to Europe to celebrate my graduation this summer . . . if . . ." His expression goes distant.

"Yeah. Sorry I asked. Let's talk about something else," I say. "Like you said your dad and Lexi's dad are business partners. What do they do?"

"They own an investment company," he says as the tide trickles closer to us.

"A what?"

Brody chuckles. "They invest in companies to get them off the ground and then they own a share."

"Really?" I ask as the water splashes over my toes.

"It's a pretty good gig." Brody grins despite himself. "But even though my dad claims that they help people, I want to do something where I really make a difference. That's why I want to go into sports medicine."

My heart leaps. That's my Brody.

"What about you, Abs? What do you want to do?"

"Well, first I want to win the scholarship." I stretch my legs out straight.

"I knew you were going to say that." He 'looks down at me, a smile spread across his face.

"You'd say it too if you were stuck working at the snack bar!"

Brody's smile narrows ever so slightly. "Abs, you've been training with me all summer. I know it's more than that."

I pause, trying to figure out what to say to him. "You know, you just got done telling me about all your elaborate vacations." I look up at him.

"Yeah, so?" He shakes his head. "I'm not really sure where you're going with this. . . ."

"Well, my 'vacations' were at the beach."

"That's nothing to be ashamed of. Beach vacations are the best."

"Yeah, they are," I begin hesitantly. "Except my beach vacations weren't in Puerto Vallarta or Antigua."

"So where did you go?"

"Exactly where the club is today." I pause, deciding how much to share. "But that was when things were good."

If Brody is horrified, he doesn't show it. "And what are things like now?"

"Now we're forced to hang out at the super crowded public beaches. Which I hate."

"Hmm . . ." Brody tilts his head, thoughtfully.

"I know. So exciting." I roll my eyes. "Let me guess: You're so shocked, you don't even know what to say."

"No, it's not that." Brody shrugs.

"Then what is it? Never dreamed your beloved club would kick people out?"

"That and I'm just thinking about what you're going to do to change things. Because you obviously don't like the beaches you're hanging at. And from what I can tell, Abigail Berkeley is one pretty determined girl."

I'm about to tell Brody that part of me has been thinking that if I win the scholarship, I might be able to improve things at the club when Brody's cell phone buzzes.

Brody digs into his pocket.

"We gotta head to the party," he says, shutting his cell.

"Who was that?" I ask.

"Lexi." He gives me a quick kiss and shoves his phone back into his pocket.

My heart pounds. Just hearing her name makes me doubt myself.

Brody gently kisses me again. Then he stands up and holds out his hand to pull me up alongside him. "It's time to announce the teams for Last Blast. We should at least show our faces."

"Wait. I thought they were going to be posted tomorrow morning at the club." I shove my feet into my flip-flops.

Brody looks at me out of the corner of his eye. "Yeah, they are. But do you really want to wait until then?" He swings his arm around my shoulder and we begin to walk around the cliff toward the group.

The second I spot the smoke from the bonfire, I maneuver away from him.

He looks at me pleadingly, but I just shake my head. I still can't bear the thought of being caught breaking Denise's rule.

"Only two more weeks until Last Blast," I remind him. I only hope that he—*and Lexi*—can keep our relationship on the DL for that long.

I trudge through the deep sand in the direction of the raging fire. Music pumps from a small DJ stand set up against the cliffs.

"Does Denise know we're here?" I ask as we approach the party. The reflection of the flames lights up Brody's face.

"Sure. She knows about the traditions. She just doesn't know when or where they take place."

Small groups of guys and girls congregate around the fire. Some chat and others jam to a club mix. A few toss wood into the bonfire, cheering when it fumes.

"Hey, Abby!" Katie yells. She's grasping a cup and dancing with Allison.

I grin and wave, feeling more at ease with each familiar face. Two guys I recognize from morning workouts roast marshmallows. A chant of *Brooke, Brooke, Brooke* rings out as a smiling Brooke appears with Greg.

"Let's party!" she shouts, holding up two cups.

I know a few non-lifeguards are allowed, but still I'm surprised to see Brooke here after what happened. And even more surprised that it seems like everyone supports them.

"I'm going to find Zoe," I say to Brody.

He nods in my direction and starts chatting with some male guards.

I spot Zoe by the DJ and run toward her, ignoring Kylie and Missy who flank her on each side. "Zoe! I've been trying to get a hold of you for, like, ever," I say.

Zoe rolls her eyes.

"Uh, Abby," Kylie mutters.

"Just one sec, Kylie," I answer, my eyes never leaving my best friend. "Zoe, I really need to talk to you."

Zoe turns her back toward me, facing the other girls.

"Wait . . . What's wrong?" I tap her shoulder.

Zoe doesn't say anything.

"Earth to Abby." Missy waves her arms.

I shake my head and am about to repeat my earlier line of questioning when I'm distracted by the sight of Brody walking up to Lexi. She nods at Brody and then calls out to the group. "Okay, it looks like everyone is finally here."

Zoe dashes away from me to join the crowd that's gathered in front of the captains—Katie and Lexi.

I follow her. "What's your problem?"

Before Zoe can answer, Lexi interrupts. "Okay, everyone please take a seat," she shouts. "We have a lot of stuff to get to tonight." Lexi clears her throat. "But first we have a very special presentation."

The crowd claps. A few lifeguards let out a cheer.

Brody and Katie carry out a white screen and place it behind Lexi.

Zoe makes her way to the opposite side of the crowd. I'm about to chase after her when Kylie and Missy pull me down to the sand.

"Abby, we have to tell you something," Missy says.

"Shh . . ." I reply. The last thing I need is to interrupt a sacred lifeguard tradition. With Lexi on my tail, I have enough to worry about.

A projector clicks on, lighting up the screen. Lexi and Brody plant themselves in front.

The DJ plays Green Day's "Time of Your Life" while photos fill the screen.

"It's important," Kylie whisper-screams to me.

Again, I shake my head, trying to focus on the shots of my co-workers as kids. It's better than watching Lexi whisper into Brody's ear.

"Abby, remember that girl we saw at the pier? The one who was hanging out with Brody?" Kylie leans over to me.

Onscreen Zoe and Zach play with a sand pail as toddlers. Katie licks an ice cream cone. Brody swims and splashes with Lexi in a blowup pool.

I face Kylie. "Yeah? Brody's sister."

"Yeah, we just found out about that connection," Missy chimes in from her spot on my other side.

"What about her?" I look back and forth between them. "Brody and I talked about her a while ago. We're all good."

A picture of a few club members at çotillion appears onscreen.

"Yeah, so she's one of Lexi's closest friends," Missy replies, a strange look of guilt on her face.

"That makes sense. Brody's dad and Lexi's dad are business partners."

The screen now fills with a shot of Lexi running. She's clearly decided that she's the star of this show.

"We didn't know that," Kylie says. "And we didn't know that she and Brody were related."

"Yeah, Missy just said that." I tilt my head, still puzzled about why we're having this conversation.

Kylie babbles on, "You should know that she goes to boarding school. She and Brody didn't used to hang out together and—"

"Wait, why are you telling me all of this?"

The crowd lets out a gasp.

"She's the one we got fired."

I turn back to the screen. An hour-old picture of Brody and me making out stares back at me.

"She's the reason why you have a job."

I run as fast as I can away from the bonfire, away from Kylie and Missy, away from Lexi and Brody, and away from the Beachwood Country Club.

# Chapter Twenty-Six

**Unfortunately, I can't stay** away from the club as long as I'd like. Snack bar duty calls the next morning. As I shine the counter, I think about how just a few weeks ago, the granite seemed so opulent. Now, it just seems like an overpriced slab.

Not that it matters what I think. I'm sure Denise knows all about my relationship with Brody by now and is heading over here to kick me off the team quicker than she can say, "Last Blast."

To make things worse, Brody hasn't called since I bolted from the bonfire. Figures that he'd disappear after we finally make out. He's no better than Nick. He got what he wanted and bailed. Exactly like my brothers predicted.

I don't have a choice anymore. I know what I'll have to tell him when I see him.

What I still can't figure out is what's going on with Zoe. The only thing I can fathom is that the club changed her into a stuck-up member just like everyone else.

"Why so glum today?" Jason slides in front of me.

I ignore him and count the swirls on the granite.

"Not talking?" Jason picks up the salt and pepper shakers. He pours a little bit from each shaker on to the palm of his hand.

I watch him lick the salt and pepper off his palm.

"That's disgusting," I say, scrunching my nose.

Jason wipes his mouth on his sleeve. "It worked. Got you talking. So, what's up?"

I continue to shine the countertop. The last thing I want to hear is another big fat *I told you so* from Jason.

Jason leans across the counter. "So, what finally clued you in to the fact that you would never break in? Was it the slideshow? Or the sentimental way that Brody and Lexi looked at each other? Oh wait, I know. It was a certain photograph."

"Wait. Were you there?" I look up.

Jason raises his left eyebrow. "Nope."

I freeze. "Is everyone talking about it?"

"Yeah, but don't worry about it." Jason knocks into me playfully. "It'll blow over."

"Jason, it won't blow over. I'm going to be kicked off the team."

"Maybe. But even if you are, at least you did a lot of good here this summer."

I snort. "What do you mean?"

"Well, you almost had me convinced that the people here weren't all that bad. That takes some doing."

I shake my head. "You should never have listened to me. You were right all along."

"I dunno. For a while there I even thought you might be able to change things."

I smile despite my mood. Then I realize what he's saying. "Okay, now you're just full of it. You never once acted like I got through to you."

"Maybe that's just because I'm 'kind of a downer.'" Jason grins at me, parroting what I said about him on my first day.

I giggle and am about to thank him for cheering me up when I hear a familiar voice pipe up behind me.

"Abs," Brody says.

My stomach tightens. I was hoping I wouldn't have to do this until later today.

"Let me know if you need me," Jason says, slowly rising from the stool. He glances at Brody and they nod at each other as each goes their separate ways.

Brody walks behind the counter and quickly kisses me on the cheek.

I lean away from him. "How's your mom?" I ask, fumbling for conversation.

"She's okay." He pauses. "The question is, are you?"

"Oh. Yeah. Fine." I begin stacking some plates.

"Abs, about last night—"

I quickly interrupt him. "Look, thanks so much for all your help and training. But I think I'm going to take it from here on my own."

"Wait. What? Because of the slideshow? I already talked to Lexi and—"

"Brody, it's not just about Lexi. Sure, I was offended by what she did. But you know? I saw it coming and I tried to ignore it." I continue stacking the plates.

Brody grabs the plates from my hands. "She still shouldn't have posted that pic."

"Yeah, we all do things we shouldn't. She shouldn't have posted that pic. You shouldn't have ignored me after I ran out. And I shouldn't have let you kiss me." I grab the plates back from him. "Training together just wasn't a good idea."

"What are you talking about?"

I hold the plates up against my chest, then let my most recent discovery stream out. "Why didn't you tell me I took your sister Mara's spot?"

"I didn't think it mattered. It was my dad who wanted her to come back here anyway, not her, and I didn't want to give you another reason not to let me train you."

"So you lied?" I squeeze the plates tighter.

"Abs, it's just that I thought that—"

"Save it." The plates clang as I drop them on the counter. I steady them with my hand and take a deep breath, gathering my thoughts. "Listen, Brody, I care about what's going on with your mom. Really, I do. And I'm still so amazed by how much you've sacrificed to help her. But just because you're a really nice guy—and you are, Brody, despite whatever happened last night . . ." My voice catches in my throat. I begin to tear up.

"Yeah?" Brody says quietly, fear and worry in his voice.

Tears slide down my cheeks. He reaches to brush them away and I jerk back, suddenly gaining strength. "I can't do this." I start to walk away.

"Abs!" Brody yells out.

"I'm sorry"—I sniffle—"but you're just not the right guy for me." I hold back the tears and turn on my heels. I don't know where I'm headed, only that it's not here.

This time, Brody trails after me. "Abs, please. Let me explain."

"Brody, I'm begging you—don't."

# Chapter Twenty-Seven

**The next two weeks** go by in a blur. And then suddenly, it's the day of the Last Blast Competition.

I can't figure out how it's happened, but miraculously I've managed to make it through without getting kicked off the team. I don't know if it's that no one's told Denise—which I doubt—or the fact that Brody and I are no longer together (in any sense of the word) or that Denise is simply waiting for the right moment, but she still hasn't said anything to me.

Still, I'm not convinced that I'm in the clear.

I've been wondering lately if my parents realize something's up. I've hardly spoken to them since my blowup with Brody and they must have noticed that I haven't exactly been seeing any friends.

But I don't have the time to worry about that. Every ounce of energy I possess is focused on winning the scholarship. I'm still desperate to change things at the club, but for now, I'll just take what I can get.

I arrive an hour and a half early for the competition, frantically hoping that Zoe is also already there. I spot her ankle deep in the ocean, chatting with Allison. She still hasn't returned any of my texts and she ignores me every time she sees me at work. I'm desperate to get her to come around, and not only because we're on the same team—the Malibu Mafia.

I slowly wade through the water, steadying myself. "Can we talk?" I ask, interrupting her conversation.

Zoe rolls her eyes. "Don't you take a hint?"

"Zo," I plead.

"I guess I better go," Allison volunteers. I don't know if she can tell how anxious I am to make things right with Zoe or if she just has better places to be, but I'm grateful for her quick departure.

"Wait up, I'm coming with you," Zoe calls out.

"Zoe, don't go," I say earnestly.

"Why shouldn't I?" She starts to trail after Allison and I grab her hand, pulling her back.

"Because you haven't talked to me in weeks, not since the bonfire where *I* was humiliated. And you won't return any of my calls or texts." My volume escalates. "You at least owe me an explanation. Why are you ignoring me?!"

"Me. Me. Me," Zoe says in a squeaky voice.

"What are you talking about?" A wave sprays my calves.

"That's all you care about this summer. Yourself!" Zoe shouts.

"That's all *I* care about? You're the one who didn't even thank me for saving her own father!" I shout back.

"Don't even go there. What about all the babysitting you were supposed to help me with this summer? Our business? But *nooo* . . . You were always busy with your super important life."

"Look, I get that you're mad that I was busy training and couldn't be there to babysit with you, but I did tell you that it would be tough juggling two jobs."

"And hanging out with Brody." Zoe pretends to check her manicure.

"And hanging out with Brody," I concur.

Zoe glances up at me, a look of satisfaction crossing her face. "Is that it? Are we done?"

"No, we're not. Not by a long shot."

Zoe crosses her arms as I soldier on.

"I tried to call you over and over again after I saved your dad. But you never returned my calls."

Zoe yawns dramatically. "There you go again."

"Huh?" At this point, I'm lost.

"Did it ever occur to you that maybe you shouldn't have even left the club without first finding me? How you should have told me about my dad in person? Checked on me? Anything?"

"It did, but—"

"But you went off with *Brody*," she says, spitting out his name.

"I tried to see if you were okay. . . ."

Zoe again rolls her eyes. "Best friends do more than call and text, Abby. But I guess you wouldn't remember that." She pauses and I can almost make out tears in her eyes. "Do you know how much you hurt me? It was *my dad*, Abby."

I'm tempted to reach out to hug her but I don't think she'd like it. "Zoe, I'm sorry. . . ." She grimaces, setting me off. "Did you ever think that maybe something was bothering me and that's why I was MIA so much?"

"There Abby goes again. Me. Me. Me." She stamps her feet, getting water all over us. "If it's 'thanks' you're looking for, thanks for being such an awesome BFF. Thanks for saving my dad. And thanks for finding the little girl who I babysit for."

I narrow my eyes, questioningly. "You've lost me. . . ."

"That little girl who you reunited with her mom? Red hair? Loves pink? She's one of the ones I babysit for."

"I didn't know. . . ."

"Of course, you didn't. You don't pay attention. Anyway, you rock. You won. Are you happy? Can I go now?" Zoe begins to walk back to shore.

"You think I've won?" I whisper, shocked at what Zoe's just told me.

"What else would you call it?"

"I'd call it being desperate to survive here. At the club, I mean."

Zoe sighs dramatically. "What are you talking about? You're one of the best swimmers the club has ever seen. Not a good friend, but . . ."

I place my hand on Zoe's shoulder. She jerks away from me right away, but at least I still have her attention. "Zo, I realize I've been completely self-absorbed lately. And I apologize for that. But there's a lot more at stake."

"I know. You're insanely in love with Brody." Zoe pretends to stick her finger down her throat. "Puke."

"A, Brody and I aren't together anymore"—Zoe's eyes widen at my big reveal, but she quickly regains her composure—"and *b*, this is about way more than any relationship that I may have previously been a part of." I gulp, concentrating on Zoe. "You'll never understand. I'm just not like you."

"I know. I'm not selfish." Zoe dramatically places her hand on her chest.

"I'm not like you because *I don't belong here.*" Zoe gives me a confused look and I continue before she can bring up any more disagreements. "You're a member. I'm not. You've gone to B-Dub your whole life. I just started. You get to replace your carpeting at a single drop of nail polish. I—"

"Nail polish? That's your big example?"

"All I'm saying is that I don't just work hard to win. I work hard to prove that I fit in." I feel a hot tear leak from my eye. "You never have to worry about that."

"That's ridiculous. Of course you fit in." Zoe motions me to the shore and we start to walk over, together this time. "You're from Malibu. Your dad and brother are cops here."

"Exactly." I pause. "Cops. How many girls do you know at Beachwood whose fathers are cops?"

Zoe's forehead furrows.

"Do you think I like hearing about how 'refreshing' my knockoff clothes are? Or how I'll sometimes have to say no to certain restaurants because I just can't afford them? Or how about how I constantly have to listen to everyone's exotic vacation plans when I'm almost always stuck at home? Not that I fault anyone—I want all of you guys to have all of that awesome stuff—I'm so thrilled for you. But it just gets upsetting after a while to always be the odd man out." I come to a stop, then tell Zoe the final truth. "And sometimes I think that the only way to ever be one of you is to win."

"I never realized you felt that way."

I inhale deeply. "I do. I always have."

**Zoe and I walk** to a lounge chair to gather her stuff before we meet up with the rest of our competition team. "So you and Brody are over, huh?" she asks now that we're on better terms.

"Yeah, I ended it." I grab a towel from the club's shelves as we walk past.

"Why would you do that?" Zoe dries off her feet.

"It was always one thing after another. . . ." My voice trails off. "Still, I can't figure out how Denise doesn't know yet. Must be a modern miracle."

"It's no miracle. The guards don't rat each other out. It's like an unwritten rule."

"Yeah, but why would anyone ever want to protect me? It sure didn't seem like Lexi was going to keep her big mouth shut." I stare at the shallow water.

"You ever guess that you're not the only one with a secret lover?"

"I dunno . . ." My voice trails off. And for a few seconds there's silence. Then I look up at Zoe. "Why are you suddenly being so nice to me?"

"What do you mean?"

"Well, you've clearly been mad at me for a long time—you stopped wearing your friendship necklace eons ago—and I didn't see it before, but you must have felt like I betrayed you."

"Yeah, I did, actually." She pauses, thinking. "But we've been friends for forever and I get it now—you had stuff of your own going on. And it was more than just about training and Brody. It was also about this stupid club that I'm a part of. So . . ."

"Yeah?" I say, my voice hopeful.

"Let's just say we're even." She playfully kicks the water, splashing me.

"Sounds good to me." I splash her back, laughing. "Now start wearing your necklace!"

Zoe stares at the empty spot around my neck. "Uh, where's yours, Miss Berkeley?" She mockingly puts her hands on her hips.

"Um . . . in my drawer at home."

Zoe raises her eyebrows.

"I didn't want to ruin it," I say guiltily.

"Okay, I'll start wearing it after the competition today on one condition."

"What's that?"

"After *you* win—"

I interrupt her. "Maybe you'll—"

She cuts me off right away. "No, Abby, don't even say it. We both know I'm not going to win." She shrugs. "Anyway, after you win the competition and the scholarship and find a way to let Brody back in—"

"I'm not going to do that."

"Right. You keep saying that. Anyway, are you gonna let me finish?"

"Fine. Sorry."

"And after we go to the Luau—and don't you even tell me about how you won't be allowed to go or make some excuse about your parents—after all that, let's remember to do things just the two of us sometimes."

"No Kylie?" I ask.

"No Kylie."

"No Missy?"

"Nope, no Missy."

I smile so widely I feel like my cheeks are about to burst. "Well, then, I'd love that!"

"Good." Zoe smiles back. "Because you didn't have a choice." She gives me a hug and I know that things between the two of us are really going to be okay. "Now let's go kick some butt!"

# Chapter Twenty-Eight

**The hazy afternoon** is more humid than hot when Zoe and I make our way to the starting line. The beach is crowded with Last Blast spectators scattered across the Beachwood Country Club grounds.

I'm shocked to see that my family even made the trip. The club must have allowed them in because of me. Still, it's so weird to see them here. Dad and Robby, looking out of place in their uniforms, stand off to the side by the cabanas. Whenever someone walks past them—even if it's just to offer them a cold beverage or an umbrella—they grimace with such intensity that passersby probably think they're protestors. Meanwhile, my mom and two other brothers have at least attempted to blend in by dressing for the beach. Still, they hold a little protest of their own, opting to sit on a towel by the volleyball nets instead of parking on the many white foldout chairs in front of the pool.

I step up to the starting line and stretch out my hamstrings. My skin prickles with excitement.

I'm dying to look at Brody for encouragement—he stands behind me in front of the tower—but I resist the urge. It doesn't matter that we're on the same team. We're over. I will myself to focus; this moment isn't about him.

"Go, Abby and Zoe!" I look over my shoulder and spot Kylie and Missy holding signs for the Malibu Mafia. I adjust my black two-piece bathing suit. I'll deal with the two of them later.

"This begins our seventh annual Last Blast Competition!" Denise shouts into a bullhorn. "The Malibu Mafia versus the Pacific Coast Pirates!"

The crowd erupts with cheers. People linger by the pool to watch the action. This is it. Everything I've worked for. I can just see the promise of college glimmering in the distance . . . if I can just manage to keep all of the club craziness out of my head—and if Lexi doesn't cheat.

"It's been another wonderful, but more importantly, safe season, thanks to the hard work of the Beachwood lifeguards. Only one save was needed this summer."

Another bout of cheers erupts and Katie looks at me, smiling. I beam back at my favorite partner and then quickly shift my gaze to Zoe, mouthing that we're in this together. There's no way that I'm going to bask in the crowd's adulation without acknowledging what she went through.

"As many of you know, two teams will be competing against each other today for the coveted Last Blast Cup." Denise points to a gleaming brass trophy that stands at attention in the middle of a table set up in front of the lifeguard tower.

As I stare at the cup, my stomach splashes around like waves during a summer storm. That cup is mine.

"The team with the most points will win the cup. And the lifeguard who earns the most points from the winning team will win an annual twenty-thousand-dollar college scholarship."

More applause rings out.

As the clapping subsides, the screech of my dad's scanner can be heard. A few gatherers glance over at my dad and whisper.

"We'll begin the competition today with the women's one-hundred-meter sand dash," Denise shouts.

I set up at the green starting line. Zoe finishes her stretches and steps beside me. She squeezes my hand.

"Good luck," she mouths.

Lexi glances my way as she shakes out her hands and legs. A burly bald man in the crowd—her father, I remember him from the invitational—screams, "Concentrate, Lex!" and her face twists. But then she quickly regains her mojo and smirks at me.

Just seeing her cocky smile sends the adrenaline rushing through my blood like a current. There's no way that Lexi Smalls is leaving here with that cup.

"Ready . . ." Denise shouts.

Lexi begins to rock into position like me.

Brody yells, "Go Mafia."

"Set."

I dig my back foot into the sand, ready to explode like a cannon. An anticipatory chill dashes up my back and runs down my legs.

"Go!" Denise shouts.

I lunge forward, feeling my muscles snap into action. With long strides, I pump my arms hard as I can. Lexi is a blur next to me. We're neck and neck. Then the first part of the competition is over as fast as it began.

I race across the finish line, stretching out my leg with the last step. Lexi is already there, a footstep ahead of me.

She slows down to a stop. Allison and her teammates surround her.

"Damn!" I turn my back to them and place my hands on my hips completely disgusted with myself. I kick the sand sending a granule shower across the beach.

After Zoe catches her breath, she finds me, holding her side. "Close . . ."

"Yeah. Great. How did you do?" I ask, pulling myself out of my pathetic pity party.

"Fifth," she answers.

I hold my hand up for a high five. "Nice, Zo."

"That's my best finish this summer," she says, grinning proudly.

"Awesome," I say, slapping her on the back.

"Yeah, look at us, earning some great points for the team," Zoe adds.

I nod in agreement and then peek at Lexi out of the corner of my eye. She's surrounded by adoring fans, many of whom aren't even from her team.

"Don't worry about them. It doesn't matter if Lexi places first in every event. It's about the team," Zoe says, pulling me out of my staring session. "Lexi won't win the scholarship if her team doesn't win."

"I had her."

She shrugs. "You'll get her in the ocean."

I glance at Lexi again. She's gone from smugly smiling and receiving congratulations from her teammates to being screamed at by her father.

"What was that? You almost lost to her!" he points to me. "Do you think that she's had half the training you've had?"

My blood boils. I'd love to tell him where he can put his precious training. I look at the volleyball net and then off to the side of the club for my own family. They don't seem thrilled, but at least they nod at me civilly.

"Go, Abby!" my mom stands up and screams. She sits back down on the towel when people start to look at her.

At least I have one fan.

Zoe grins at me, grabbing a water bottle off a refreshment table manned by Jason. "Like I said, it doesn't matter." She runs off to talk to her mom.

Jason tosses me a bottle. "Nice race," he says

"Yeah, right," I say, twisting the cap off.

As I'm drinking, I feel someone gently brush up against me. I look up and see that it's Brody. He's also come to grab a water bottle. I can't tell though if he rubbed against me by accident or on purpose. He looks at me earnestly and says my name, "Abs," in a single breath.

I glance at my parents, then Denise, and then back at him. The competition isn't over yet.

"Not here," I say. I swallow and walk away.

\* \* \*

**"That cup is ours!"** Zoe screams as we slap hands about an hour later. She steps behind me before the scenario save, the second girls' event of the day.

"Victims in distress, take your mark!" Denise shouts through her bullhorn.

The lifeguards not participating in the competition jog into the ocean to act as victims. I adjust my swim cap and pull at my bathing suit, snapping it against my skin. I look down at my goose bump–covered legs as I wait for the "victims" to set up.

With two events left, Lexi's team is up by two points after their guys also won the sand dash. The pressure is on.

The victims line up horizontally next to the bobbing flags. They begin waving for help.

I look over at Lexi's team. Of course, Lexi, like me, is set up to save. Her teammate, Allison, stands behind her ready for the victim lift.

"Set," Denise screams.

The rope dangles across my body, fluttering in the wind.

*ERNNNN* . . .

The horn sounds and I take off. I hear the cheers as I dive head-first into the first wave. Then, boom.

Bubbles and the comforting silence of the ocean.

I emerge, then re-submerge, diving like a dolphin until I clear the waves. Immediately I begin the freestyle stroke, finding a similar rhythm as I did back in May when I won the invitational. I reach our victim, Tammi, within seconds and toss her the buoy. I signal to Zoe, treading water. When I know Tammi's secure, I begin my swim back to the sand.

Tammi's pull yanks me back a few feet. Once I can stand on the sand, I begin to use the waves to my advantage, working them one-by-one. Like clockwork, Zoe sprints to my side. Together we use the rope to pull Tammi to shore. As soon as Tammi is in shallow water, I set up in front. Here we go.

"One. Two. Three. Pick up," Zoe shouts.

I maneuver Tammi's arms to balance on my shoulders. Then I hoist Tammi's upper body onto my back as Zoe lifts her lower half. We take off to the finish line running like we're in a wheelbarrow race.

"Come on, Allison!" Lexi screams next to us.

"Mafia, by a mile!" Denise screams into the bullhorn.

The beach erupts into cheers.

Zoe and I gingerly lower Tammi.

"Nice job, guys," Tammi says, as she grabs a towel.

Behind her, Lexi's dad grabs her by the arm and pulls her to the side of the crowd. He resumes his pointing and screaming.

I spot Brody grabbing a buoy by the tower and mouth, "Thank you." We might be a thing of the past, but I still owe a lot to my trainer.

Brody nods, then says audibly, "It's all you."

**"On your marks!"** Denise shouts.

The butterflies in my stomach fight for position as I stare at the orange two-hundred-meter flag flapping in the wind. We're tied with Lexi's team after six events, thanks in part to Brody's coming in first during the men's save event. It's finally the last women's race—the ocean swim—and it's all up to me to bring it home.

"Get set!" The wind whips, throwing me off balance for a second. I position my feet on the wet sand, pull my goggles over my eyes, and suck in a breath, concentrating on getting into my zone.

"Go!"

The crowd roars behind me as my feet slap across the shallow water. I tear across the shin-deep waves, ignoring Lexi's father as he yells out instructions. The other guards splash me as they run, but I pay them no attention. Once the water is waist height, I hold my breath and surface dive underneath a breaker.

Silence.

I emerge and begin my freestyle over the waves, the other guards jockeying for spots beside me. I find my breath while keeping my head above water and quickly get into a rhythm. I stretch my arms as far out as possible, attempting to gain as much mileage as I can. I smile as I feel myself pull away from the pack.

I spot another wave about to break, so I hold my breath and fight it with all my strength, refusing to allow the momentum to thrust me back to the shore. Brody's words echo in my mind as I use my kick to drive me forward across the rough salty water. The flag is within feet.

With the wicked waves assaulting me, my freestyle isn't perfect. But my strong kick gives me enough power to propel myself toward the flag.

I swim past a paddleboat manned by a male lifeguard, and I'm surprised when he yells out, "You're in the lead!"

Those words act like an extra shot of adrenaline. I swim around the flag, pulling my body to the surface of the water to resume my freestyle. My lungs burn as I chop the water, moving closer to the shore with each motion. With the current at my back, the swim to shore is smoother and easier than the swim out to the flag.

*Whoosh.*

I allow the massive wave to push me to shore. When it's about to crest, I surface dive. Then I feel for the bottom with my feet. A piece of slimy seaweed wraps around my ankle as my toes touch the sand.

*Bingo.*

I begin sprinting through the shallow water. And then out of nowhere, a rush of water pelts me from behind. But I don't dare look. I know it's Lexi gaining on me.

Lexi uses her hands to push for position. I push back. All eyes are on us as we dash toward the finish line.

"Lexi! Lexi! Lexi!" the crowd chants.

"Use your power!" Lexi's dad yells. His pacing is visible even through my goggle-blurred vision.

And then a few more voices add themselves to the chorus. "You got it, Abby!" my dad bellows.

"Be tough, Abs!" Brody shouts.

I don't let myself think about either of them.

I pump my arms, feet from the finish. Suddenly, I realize that there's no way I'm going to win on foot. I stretch out and dive across the finish line like I'm sliding home headfirst.

For a second, everything is a blur, and then I hear Denise's voice echo from the bullhorn. "Abby Berkeley is the winner by a hair!" she shouts.

It might be my imagination, but it feels like the crowd goes silent for a moment. Then applause roars and the crowd, which had previously been chanting Lexi's name, starts yelling mine.

I pull off my goggles and swim cap, tossing them to the side. I look around in awe—I'd been working for this moment for so long it's totally surreal now that it's here.

My sense of wonderment comes to an abrupt end when I feel someone jump on my back.

"You did it!" Zoe says, smacking my back.

Just then, a towel is tossed at my face.

I look up in the direction it came from and there's Jason, smiling and giving me the thumbs-up.

*Huh. Maybe I really did change his mind about how things could be here.*

"You look like a sand monster." Zoe points to the grains covering the entire front of my body.

I use the towel Jason threw at me to wipe away the rough sand.

As soon as I'm done, Zoe grabs my towel and comes in for a high five. "Who's gonna be the scholarship winner? Abby Berkeley's gonna be the scholarship winner." She moves her head from side to side.

I giggle. "We still have to wait for the men's event."

"Nah. It's in the bag," says a new voice.

I look to my right and am surprised to see that Katie has come over to congratulate me. "I have to say I'm seriously impressed, part-ner." She slaps me on the back. "In all my years at the club, I've never seen a performance like that. Way to go!"

"Excuse me!" I hear a husky voice call out. I look over and see that Brody has cut through the crowd and is practically running toward me. He looks like he's about to scoop me up into his arms, but then we make eye contact and he stops mid-stride, suddenly remembering where things stand between us. For a second, he just stands there, staring at me, as if he can't decide whether our recent reconciliation means he's allowed to approach me as anything more than my trainer.

I shake my head—I don't want him to get any ideas—but inside my heart screams for him.

He buries his head in my neck. "I knew you could do it," he whispers.

Oh. My. God.

"Are they still together?" I hear Katie whisper to Zoe.

Zoe whispers back, "Once Abby decides to get her head out of her butt."

"Men, you're up in five minutes!" Denise yells in the distance.

Katie and Zoe wave at me, walking off to watch the upcoming race.

Brody pulls away from my neck and looks me straight in the eyes. "You're gonna win the scholarship, Abs. You carried us. You're amazing."

My eyes plead for him to kiss me, to forget about everything I said about us being wrong for each other. "Friends . . ." I murmur, more to myself than to him. "We can be friends."

Brody hangs his head. "Yeah, friends . . ." He lingers for a moment and then takes off toward his mark.

"So that's him, huh?" my dad asks, startling me. He pats me on my damp hair.

"Yup," I weakly reply. Then a lightening bolt rips through my stomach. "Wait, no. Dad, it's over. Don't say any—"

"It's over? Why would it be over?" My dad raises his eyebrows.

"He came up to talk to me. Seems like a smart boy. Told me I have an amazing daughter. Knows a good thing when he sees it."

My heart flutters. I can't believe Brody told my father that. I watch as Brody takes his mark at the starting line and am suddenly filled with a sense of pride—that's my sort of ex-boyfriend slash trainer person out there.

Looking around, I notice that Lexi and her dad have disappeared. The crowd meanwhile has refocused its attention on the upcoming race. I gulp. Clearly, I was just a quick blip on the collective radar. I turn back to my dad. "It's just that we're too different."

My dad places his hand on my shoulder. "There are worse things in life, Abigail."

"Huh?" I furrow my brow in confusion.

"Homicides, MVAs, natural disasters . . ."

"That's great," I say, sighing. "I feel so much better."

"You know, I'm very proud of you," he adds, squeezing my shoulder tighter.

"Thanks, Dad," I say, wrapping my towel around my shoulders as I allow his words to wash over me.

Unfortunately, I can't relish in the rare moment of father-daughter understanding for long because, of course, that's when the rest of my family chooses to come over.

"Was that cutie Brody?" my mom asks. She means well, but as soon as my response—"Yup, that's Brody"—is out, it's an invitation for my brothers to pile on.

"Do you want me to tell him to keep his hands off you?" Robby asks, stepping forward with his arms crossed tightly across his chest.

"Will you guys just relax?" I say, my volume rising.

"He mentioned something about going to college anyway when I was talking to him earlier," Frankie adds.

My stomach drops. "You talked to him too?"

Alex continues where Frankie left off. "Yeah and you know what guys do when they go to college."

"Will you guys just shut up for once? Brody's not like that."

Frankie rolls his eyes.

"Yeah sure," Alex interjects.

Robby follows up with, "All freshman guys are like that."

"Oh my God!" I yell. "When are you going to stop trying to run my life?"

"Honey, they're just overprotective. You know how brothers are. They just want to make sure you're safe. That's all," my mom's calm voice interrupts my tantrum. "They feel like they're losing you to all this."

I look from my brothers to my dad. "Is that true?"

My dad looks at my mom.

"Of course it's true," she says. "This is a new world for them. All this glitz and glam. They're worried that the Abby we know and love is just going to *poof!* disappear."

"I'm not going anywhere," I say, wrapping my arm around my dad's shoulder. "I can be part of all this—lifeguard here, go away to college—and still be a Berkeley."

"I know, Nemo," he says, looking down at me. "It's just going to take me a little while."

I hug my dad.

Then I look at my brothers. "So what's the deal with you

boneheads? You really just afraid your little sister is gonna get too classy for you?"

"Yeah, that *is* what we're worried about," Alex says guiltily.

"But never fear!" Frankie calls out. "We have our ways of making sure you'll always be a woman of the people." He snatches me up in a choke hold and gives me a noogie.

Robby grabs my legs.

"Boys. I don't think this is the right time and place for horse-play," my mom says.

Alex grabs my arms, then waves my parents off.

I wiggle, but it's no use. My brothers firmly have me in their grasp. They walk me down to the ocean edge, a few hundred feet away from where the men's competition is still going on.

"Ready!" Frankie yells.

"No!" I shout, knowing what's coming.

They begin to swing me.

"No, guys. Please!" I plead.

They laugh maniacally. "One, two, three!" they all yell in unison and toss me into a wave.

I shut my eyes tight and hold my nose as I smash into the huge wave. My butt skids across a sand bar.

When I eventually stand up, I shout, "You guys are dead!"

"You'll never get us!" they yell, taking off across the sand.

I glance at the members of the competition audience who've caught sight of what we're doing. I shrug—whatever. Then I take off after my brothers.

\* \* \*

**"It's time to announce** the winner of this year's Last Blast Competition!" Denise calls out after the crowd has taken their seats on the white folding chairs now set up along the beach. In front of the tower, a stage has been constructed for the announcement.

She pulls a folded piece of paper out of her pocket. Unfolding it, she gazes out at the audience from her spot on the podium. Then she looks down at the paper and speaks into the microphone, "With thirty-one points out of her team's seventy-six total, this year's scholarship winner and next year's captain is Abigail Berkeley!"

The crowd erupts. Chants of "Abby! Abby! Abby!" sound out with more excitement than I knew that the onlookers had in them. As I make my way to the podium, I glance at Zoe and my parents, thrilled to finally be in a good place with everyone who's important to me.

Just then, Brody whistles. My stomach drops. *Okay, so not everyone . . .*

Fortunately, it's not more than twenty seconds later before Denise says, "We would like to present Abigail Berkeley with the Last Blast trophy and scholarship to the school of her choice." She hands me the gleaming gold trophy.

I feel a hot tear fall from my eye as the crowd roars in applause.

Denise hands me an envelope. "Congratulations," she whispers. Then to everyone else she says, "Congratulations go out to Abby and her team, the Malibu Mafia."

I stare at the scholarship envelope in one hand and the trophy in the other. Then I hear Zoe yell out, "Yeah Abby!"

At that moment, everything I've been through since the first time Zoe and I stepped on this very sand two and a half months ago comes barreling back to me like an unexpected wave.

I take a deep breath and glance at Denise.

She nods, reminding me it's time for my speech.

The crowd claps in anticipation.

I clear my throat. "First, I want to thank the Beachwood Country Club for this honor today."

More applause.

"But this win today isn't just about me." I look at Zoe, then at my brothers. "This is for every girl out there—regardless of where you live or what you come from—who dreams of becoming a lifeguard. Everyone deserves the opportunity."

A hush rolls across the crowd. They know I'm about to do something to rock the boat.

I steel my nerves and continue. "And that's why I think that everyone who dreams of working this beach should have the chance to try out for a spot on the lifeguard team, regardless of whether they or their parents are club members."

The crowd is so silent that you could hear a pin drop.

"So for my first act as captain, I hereby make the Beachwood Country Club lifeguard tryouts open to all!"

No one moves. Then my parents and brothers begin to clap. And then out of nowhere, I hear Brody start to chant, "Open try-outs! Open tryouts!" It's not long before the other lifeguards join in, "Open tryouts! Open tryouts!"

Most of the members look around at each other in confusion, though a few do clap politely.

Denise grabs the microphone from me, taking this as her cue. "Okay. Well, thanks, Abby." She pauses and looks out at the crowd nervously. "Well, that concludes today's Last Blast Competition. Drive safely." Placing her hand over the microphone, she turns to me. "This will have to go through the board, you know."

"I know." I shrug.

"But I have to say that I like your gumption." She winks at me, then steps off the podium.

My team surrounds me as soon as she leaves.

Katie wraps her arm around my shoulders. "Congratulations, captain," she says.

"Yeah. Congrats," Zoe says. "Although I knew you could do it. Because . . ."

"I know," I say. "Abby always wins."

Zoe beams. "Exactly."

I notice that Brody is standing back by the chairs, away from the rest of the group. His ear-to-ear grin is visible even from this distance.

I'm about to walk over to him when my dad climbs up onto the stage. "Phenomenal speech, Abigail," he says. "I was proud of you before, but after that, I couldn't be more humbled by you than I am today." I could be wrong but I think I spot a few tears in his eyes.

"Way to go, sweetheart," my mom says, sniffling as she envelopes me. Unlike my dad, she doesn't try to hide that she's been crying.

Once my mom steps away, my brothers crowd around me. As they jostle for my attention, I can make out what looks to be a really uncomfortable scene a few rows away. Lexi and her dad have returned from wherever they fled, but they don't appear to have made peace in the interim. If anything, it looks like the situation has only grown worse. She pleads with him as he hangs his head in disappointment. Her mother, meanwhile, is nowhere to be seen.

"Look," My father says, drawing my attention back to my family. "We realize how much all this means to you—lifeguarding here, going to college. And as much as we don't like the club . . ."

"All we want is for you to be happy," my mom says, picking up where my dad trailed off.

"Yeah, and because of that, we won't stand in your way," Robby adds, resting his hands on his leather belt.

"You won't?"

"Well, unless some jerk tries to mess with you," Frankie smirks.

"And speaking of jerks—"

"Alex, watch the language," my mom cuts him off.

"And speaking of guys in your life," Alex continues. "There's a certain one with a weird name standing over there, waiting to talk to you." He points behind me.

I turn and see that Brody is still standing there, just as he has been ever since people first started coming over to congratulate me. Tons of people float past him, but he doesn't acknowledge them. His eyes stay glued on me.

I wave at him vigorously before I even know what I'm doing; it's like my hand has a mind of its own. I quickly put my hand down, my stomach dropping. Logically, I know that I can't be captain and date Brody—although I might be able to break barriers when it comes to non-members, I'll never convince Denise to break the no-fraternizing policy—but in that moment, I realize that to give up one would be to give up a part of myself.

Brody smiles at me earnestly, inviting me to start anew with him, to begin again in a world free from silly rules and worries.

I swallow a lump. There's no such place.

# Chapter Twenty-Nine

**"Are you sure** you want to do this?" Jason asks as we arrive at the club later that night. At least three carloads of his friends—all fellow BCC employees, none of them club members—pull up behind us.

"Absolutely," I say. "I meant everything I said during my acceptance speech." We're a good half hour late for the Luau. It's time for the club to start accepting change.

"Okay," Jason shrugs.

The valet is dressed for the occasion in an ivory-and-teal flowered Hawaiian shirt. He hesitates before he opens the door for me and my guests.

"Please," I say to him.

He furrows his brow. "I guess it's okay. . . ."

I beam at him. "Thank you! Thank you!"

Jason wraps his arm around my shoulders in a brotherly fashion.

Turning to the valet, he says, "You just made her special day that much better." He pauses. "And ours."

I feel like I'm glowing. *How is this the same grumpy Jason that I worked with all summer?*

As soon as the valet opens the door to the lobby, I'm immediately assaulted by Hawaiian music.

"Look at this place!" a girl yells.

Tiki torches surround the pool, giving off streams of black smoke.

"This is insane," another guy remarks.

He's not wrong—there are more tropical flowers than I ever thought existed.

As luck would have it, Lexi is the first person I spot. She's dressed in a flowing Michael Kors floral dress and is deep in conversation with Brody. Of course. After what Brody told me, I doubt if there's really anything there, but I guess she's trying to win at least once today.

I spot a lei dangling over the marble fountain statue. I grab it and hang it around Katie's neck as I pass her.

"Thanks!" she exclaims, taking a break from chatting with one of the older male guards. "I've been looking for one of those."

I hear Zoe screech, "Abby! You came!"

A second later, I'm surrounded by Zoe, Kylie, and Missy, all with flowers in their free-flowing hair and extra leis in their hands. Kylie fluffs my hair.

"We forgiven?" Missy asks, holding up the assortment of leis. "We brought gifts!"

Kylie rolls her eyes at her. "We're really sorry about what we did," she adds sincerely. "We had no idea she was . . ."

"Yeah, yeah, of course." I shrug. There's no point in being mad at them any longer. It's not their fault how things worked out. Looking at Kylie, I say, "I know you were going through a rough patch." Then I turn to Missy, giggling. "You, on the other hand, had no excuse."

She grins back, "Nope. *Mea culpa.*" She places a pink lei around my neck. "Token of my apology," she says.

As she rests the lei around me, the group of them catch sight of Jason's friends behind me. "What is that?" Missy asks.

"Oh my God, Abby. How many people did you bring with you?" Zoe asks, pushing Kylie out of the way.

"A lot."

"They look familiar. Who are they?" Kylie asks.

I raise my eyebrows. "You should know: they're all club employees, Jason's friends. Consider this my second official act as captain."

"You're my hero," Missy says, coming at me with her lip-gloss wand. Then she sighs. "So many new hotties. So little time."

Kylie and Zoe pretend to swoon.

Just then, the DJ replaces the Hawaiian songs with club beats. He smiles at us as he mixes the tunes. Everyone begins to dance, and if the members didn't notice that there were party crashers before, they sure do now.

Fortunately, no one seems to care. Even Brooke and Allison shrug and join in on the fun, pulling me to the center.

"This is awesome!" Zoe yells as she joins the group. She drags a crowd, including Kylie and Missy, around me.

Missy does the running man dance with a crazy face next to a guy Jason brought, causing us to crack up. The guy then takes this as his cue to start break dancing.

"Best summer eva!" Zoe yells.

Missy, Kylie, and I cheer.

Kylie wraps her arm around my shoulders and squeezes.

As I'm dancing, I feel a light tap on my shoulder.

When I turn around, I see that it's Lexi.

"Can I talk to you for a sec?" she asks. Her eyes dart from me to the crowd.

I shrug and follow her to a spot behind the lifeguard tower. "What's up?"

"I just wanted to say that I didn't actually want to get you in trouble or anything." She looks up at the star-filled sky.

"Is that your 'I'm sorry'?" I ask, eyeing the party. Only a few seconds with Lexi and already I'm itching to get back.

"Yeah, I guess. Look. I'm sure you saw at the competition that my dad is crazy. He puts a ton of pressure on me. Plus, you heard about my friend Mara who got fired. . . ."

"Yeah, I did."

"Well, I kind of blamed you for it, you and your friends . . ." Her voice trails off. "Brody doesn't care about it, you know. His sister didn't even like guarding here. She's using the free time to do some filmmaking on the fly. But I was offended and I've got other stuff going on in my life that my parents won't exactly be thrilled with when they find out."

I hold up my hand. "It's fine, Lex. We all have our stuff."

Lexi smirks. "Okay. Great. Then we're cool?"

"Sure. I guess."

And with that, she walks away.

When I turn around to rejoin the crowd, Brody is in front of me. Shivers run down my spine. He lifts my chin with his index finger, looks deep into my eyes, and says, "You know that deal we made this afternoon? About being friends?"

"Yeah . . ." My stomach fills with butterflies.

"Well, I can't be friends with you anymore."

I shirk back. "What? But . . . I . . . ."

"This is my last summer at Beachwood."

My feet lose feeling. "Where are you going? Michigan? Is your mom better?"

"I got a job guarding at the UCLA gym. It's not the beach, but it works."

"You did?" I feel my heart swell. "So you got accepted to UCLA?"

"Not yet. But I'm hoping this is a step in the right direction. For my future and for me and you."

*Wait, what!?*

He runs the back of his hand along my arm. "So what went wrong after the bonfire? I know I didn't find you till the next morning and everything and I'm sorry about that. But I figured that if I got another job and wasn't working here, that would mean that you wouldn't have to worry about the rule anymore and—"

I don't know if it's the luau or what Brody just told me, but I grab him and kiss him hard. Right there in front of everyone.

At first, he's surprised, but then he grabs me tightly around my waist and pulls me closer. He tastes sweet like pineapple juice. My feet lift off the ground as we find our rhythm. When he gently lowers me back to the sand, we hear cheers behind us.

"Finally!" Zoe shouts.

I laugh, but I don't let it get to me. I know she means well.

Brody whispers in my ear, sending chills down my back. "I don't know if I'm going to be able to let you go back to school in a few days. We missed out on so much time."

I stare into his deep green eyes. "Well, then it's good that we have now, isn't it?" I jump into his arms and we kiss again as the waves crash behind us.

In the distance, we hear cheering. Then Brody and I watch a group of people sprint toward the ocean. Once they reach the water, they tumble into the waves. As they come up, I get a better view of who led them, hand-in-hand—Lexi and Jason.

My jaw drops. Slowly, a picture starts to form in my mind: Lexi telling me she had things that she couldn't tell her parents about; Jason getting so mad at her, irrationally so; the way she looked at him the first time she saw him at the snack bar; how she was always trying to get his attention; how Denise's rule prevented lifeguards from dating *all* club employees; how bitter Jason was . . . before. "So Lexi and Jason were together this entire summer?" I look up at Brody.

"They broke up right before the summer started. Lexi's idea. But the two of them were perfect for each other. I've been telling her that all along."

I watch as Lexi and Jason make out as they bob up and down beneath the waves. The rest of the party splashes around, giggling.

"Well, good for them," I exclaim. "We shouldn't be the only ones to be this lucky."

"Captain Abby Berkeley, you are amazing," Brody says.

"I try." I wink, wrapping my arms around Brody's neck. "You know, I was looking forward to bossing you around next summer. So much for that."

I go in for another kiss.

Brody lifts me up in the air. Then with me in his arms, he plants the most amazing kiss on my lips as the beach waves wash over his feet.

Zoe was right: sophomore summer was the best ever.

# Acknowledgments:

**First and foremost,** thanks to the prettyTOUGH readers and fans of the series, booksellers, librarians, and the amazing group of bloggers I've had the honor of meeting through e-mails, posts, and in person. I cherish each and every one of our correspondences and I cannot express in words how much your encouragement and kudos mean to me.

Thank you to Jane Schonberger and George Morency for not only creating this amazing brand for athletic girls but for dedicating your lives to it. Also, thanks for your hospitality and for making my family and me feel so at home in Los Angeles this summer. The trip was an amazing experience we'll never forget.

Thanks to everyone at Razorbill for your guidance and incredibly hard work. Thanks to Gillian Levinson, my talented and hardworking editor. This book wouldn't be close to what it is without you. Also, bunches of thanks to Michelle Grajkowski, my fairy agent (or super agent as Kaci calls you), for your never-ending encouragement and cheers. I'm so blessed to work with such an incredible team.

This book would not be possible without the beta reads and critiques from Katia Raina, Kari Olson, Carrie Harris, Colleen Rowan Kosinski, and Jane Schonberger. Thanks so much for your prettyTOUGH comments and for pushing me to be a better writer. A special thanks to my lifeguard expert, Annamaria Colella, for reading early drafts and answering tons of questions about everything from sneakers on the beach to swim competitions.

As always thanks bunches to my family for picking up the slack and cheering me on. Mom, your strength is always an inspiration to me. And Dad, thanks for the police jargon, insight, and trips in your squad car. The father depicted in the book is not you. You're too kind, strong, sane, and accepting. Ron, Ida, Kelly, Michael, Nicole, and Anthony, thanks bunches for all your cheers and help with childcare. To my niece, Sydney, thanks for your list of character names and for keeping me company while I write. Thanks to my youngest niece, Sabrina, for reading *Stealing Bases* out loud to me for the first time. I'm so proud of both of you.

And last but certainly not least, thanks to my incredible tribe, Justin and Kaci Olivia. Justin, without your encouragement I would be talking about writing a book without ever actually doing it. Thanks for picking up the slack while I'm on deadline, listening to my first drafts, and offering up your boy dialogue suggestions. And last, but certainly not least, thanks to my daughter, Kaci Olivia. You give me the courage to write what I love and to be my authentic self. You're my inspiration, Boo. I love you both bunches.

*Making Waves* was written in memory of Tina Voiro, a prettyTOUGH girl with a kind and generous heart who was taken from this world suddenly during the initial drafting stage of this novel. A charity, Healing Hearts: The Tina Voiro Foundation Inc., was created in this amazing woman's memory. It raises funds to donate Automated External Defibrillators to youth sports organizations.